THE CROSS AND THE SWORD

Hoi Chu Thap Va Thanh Kiem

Perry McMullin

iUniverse, Inc.
Bloomington

The Cross and the Sword
Hoi Chu Thap Va Thanh Kiem

iUniverse books may be ordered through booksellers or by contacting:

iUniverse
1663 Liberty Drive
Bloomington, IN 47403
www.iuniverse.com
1-800-Authors (1-800-288-4677)

ISBN: 978-1-4759-4231-6 (sc)
ISBN: 978-1-4759-4246-0 (hc)
ISBN: 978-1-4759-4230-9 (e)

Library of Congress Control Number: 2012914443

Printed in the United States of America

iUniverse rev. date: 08/17/2012

The Cross and the Sword is dedicated to all Vietnam veterans and to those who are serving the United States of America in her armed forces today. From day one to present, those going to war never have a good day, especially not a prisoner of war (POW).

The best friend an old corps marine could ever have, Captain Nathan D. Jacobs. I will see you on the other side skipper!

TeeeenHuuut! Preeeesent Arrrrms! Reeeeady Toooo!

I salute you!

Introduction

The Cross and the Sword (Hoi Chu Thap Va Thanh Kiem) is a fictional book that is based on some actual events. While consideration was given to accuracy and the represented timeline, this author has taken considerable artistic license in writing *The Cross and the Sword*. This book is not intended to be biographical by any stretch of the imagination, nor is it intended to be historic in nature.

Some of the names found in this book are engraved on the Vietnam Veterans Memorial Wall. I have done this to salute these warriors, and I hope that none of us will ever forget these brothers and sisters.

Of the 58,267 names that are etched on the black wall of honor, twelve of those listed as killed in action were ultimately found to be alive. Sixteen chaplains' names are also on the wall. Of the 7,484 brave women who served in Vietnam, there were nine deaths.

The pictures that grace the front and back covers of this book are some of Perry McMullin's original photographs that he made at the wall one morning, just after first light.

Thank you to Bob French for providing me with the concept for this book. The two of us sat and imagined for many hours, bringing this fiction book to fruition.

Semper Fi and a hand salute to Gunnery Sergeant Carlos Hathcock. He was, in fact, the best of the best, and no fiction book could ever be better than his true life story.

In this book, I have used the names of four Medal of Honor winners, all marines. I am damn proud to have actually served with Peter S. Connor (KIA[1]) and Jay Vargas (WIA[2]). I was personally a part of the honor guard for Ronald Coker (KIA) upon his internment at Alliance, Nebraska. James Anderson Jr. (KIA) is the first black marine to be awarded the Medal of Honor. Please be aware that I used their names *only to honor* these men; they *did not* serve in the capacity that I wrote them into in my book, however.

Fair winds and following seas!
Cong bang suc giova bien sau!

---

[1] Killed in action
[2] Wounded in action

TERMS and TERMINOLOGY from Marines in VIETNAM

A-CARD: Also known as the "ticket." This was to show your qualification or requalification on any weapon or weapon system.

ACQUIRED: Also known as "procured," but never as stolen, which it probably was. The most preferable source of *acquiring* something was from another branch of service. Nothing was ever too big or too small for a marine to *acquire*.

ADMIN: Administrative office.

AGENT ORANGE: The better known of the dioxins but less potent than the agents *purple, pink,* and *green.* Also used were agents *blue* and *white.* The names are derived from the wide-colored bands that were painted on the containers to identify the chemicals. The color of the agents themselves was not actually blue, pink, green, etc.

AGGRESSORS: These are marines that become the pretend enemy for other marines in drills. The bad guys wore a different-looking uniform but they still cheated like marines are known to (sometimes) do.

AK-47: A Soviet assault rifle capable of firing six hundred rounds per minute. Designed by Russian Mikhail Kalashnikov in the late forties, this is a superb weapon that is still being used successfully all over the world.

ARC LIGHT: The well-known code name for an air strike provided by the B-52 heavy bomber. The enemy called them *lm lang chet tu tren cao,* or silent death from above. See also **B-52.**

ARVN: "Army Republic of Vietnam" soldier. They were the ones that were supposed to be on our side. They were much less enthusiastic about the war than we were.

ATTITUDE: Issued to all marines at some time and place. It is always possible to tell a former marine ... not much; but you can tell them! We try to be subtle about being the best there is however.

B-52: A heavy or large bomber that was initially designed in the late forties to deliver a nuclear payload during the Cold War. The B-52D saw service in Vietnam under the code name Arc Light. This aircraft carries a payload of 60,000 pounds, or about 240 bombs, each one weighing 250 pounds. The aircraft was affectionately known as BUFF, as in big ugly fat fellow, or big ugly fat fucker.

BA MUOI BA: Vietnamese for the number thirty-three. This was the local beer of poor quality. The good news was there was nothing living that swam in it. The bad news was that it tasted pretty bad. See also **Tiger Piss.**

BEAUCOUP: Pronounced *boo-coo*. A French word meaning a lot of something.

BFR: "Big fucking rock." For example, no aircraft should ever become a BFR

BOHICA: "Bend over, here it comes again."

BOOGIE: To get away from a place quickly. You could also say "to haul ass."

BOOT: It could be the thing on your foot, but generally a marine that was either just out of boot camp or someone that was new to a location or a job. If you were even newer than a boot, you were a "shower shoe."

BROKEN ARROW: Worse than a last-resort radio call. "Broken arrow" will bring all friendly fire and air support directly onto your own location. This was only called when your position was being overrun and you wanted to take as many of them with you as possible. These were last words that were ever spoken by true heroes.

BURNED: To have been seen, caught, found or observed.

BUSH, BOONIES, BRUSH, or BOONDOCKS: Out and away from most people, houses, humans, etc.

BUTTER BAR: A new second lieutenant. They are called a "butter bar" because the rank insignia is gold, as opposed to a first lieutenant's bar being silver.

CO: Commanding officer.

CHAPLAIN: Religious officer providing the needs and services for marines, which are provided by the navy.

CHARLIE: The Viet Cong—guerilla type of warfare as opposed to the regular NVA. They may have been unsophisticated, but they were very formidable.

CHIEU HOI: This was a largely unsuccessful program to encourage defections. Some people defected three or more times because we gave them a cash reward each time. *Chieu hoi* translates to "open arms." To say that this program was not thought out very well would be an understatement.

CHUCK: Black marines called white marines chuck, or sometimes cracker. I never thought of it as a racial thing, it was more of a brotherhood. We all bled the same color. See also **SPLIB.**

CLAYMORE: The M-18 Claymore mine is a concave, command-detonated, directional, fragmentation device containing approximately seven hundred steel spheres. It will ruin your day!

CORPSMAN: A paramedic with combat boots. Medical services are provided by the navy, but to say that these men (women didn't serve in the field) would be a gross understatement. Corpsmen are revered by marines.

COVERED: For starters, your cover is your hat. In the navy and marines, you must remove your cover when indoors unless you are under arms (armed).

DA NANG: Located in the I ("Eye") Corps area of South Vietnam. During the war, Vietnam was divided into I, II, III, and IV Corps. Da Nang was a major air base for all branches of the US Forces as well as the **ARVN** and **VNAF**.

DIOXIN: Primarily used as a herbicide and defoliant. Agents purple, pink, green and orange were all used in Vietnam. Agents white and blue did contain dioxin.

DOC: Corpsman for navy, coast guard and marine corps, medic for army and airforce

DOD: Department of Defense. The DOD, CIA, NIS, etc., were all engaged in covert operations in Vietnam. See also **Spook**.

DOPE: The elevation and windage applied to the rifle sights to have the bullet strike where you want. Be it at seventy-five meters or five hundred meters, you have to adjust for the distance and the wind.

DUST OFF: The radio call sign for medical-evacuation helicopters in Vietnam.

E-CLUB: The enlisted club for private, private first class and lance corporal's. There was also the NCO club for corporal and sergeants, the staff NCO club for E-7 through E-9. Then of course there was also the officers club.

ETA: "Estimated time of arrival." Not to be confused with FTA, which was "fuck them all." Close in letters but very different in meaning.

FIGMO: "Fuck it, got my orders." You became a short-timer at one week left in country, unless you were a grunt. They got short when they sat inside the freedom bird to finally come home. Frequently grunts climbed aboard the freedom bird with wet mud on their boots.

FIREBASE: An outpost of varying sizes, support, artillery, air strip, and numbers of personnel. They were all dirty, nasty, primitive, and lacking in everything except for *valor!*

FIVE-BY-FIVE: Used by communications (comm) people. Before the fancy radio equipment the marines have today we still used the AN/PRC 10, FM radio. This radio came out in 1951 and it was still in use (with me) in 1965. When asked, "How do you copy (hear) this station?"; you'd reply "Five-by-five," if they were loud and clear.

FEET WET: Ditching or crashing into the ocean. To some that flew off of carriers, it just meant that they were now flying over the ocean.

FIRE-WATCH RIBBON: The National Defense Ribbon or medal. It is earned while in boot camp so it was of little or no consequence to anyone except those who only had that one ribbon.

FLASH RADIO TRAFFIC: Emergency or high-priority traffic. Everyone else … shut up!

FLICK or FLIC: Movie.

GREEN MACHINE: Another endearing name for the Marine Corps. The least flattering was probably "The Crotch."

GOOK: A derogatory and ethnic slur referring to Asians. The term has been traced to US Marines serving in the Philippines around 1920. Also used are *slope, slope head, zipper-head, dink, slant-eyes, slants, gomers, goners,* and several other "endearing" names.

GRENADE FENCE: A heavy wire mesh that covered the entire front of a building. It had a slanted top so a hand grenade or other explosive device wouldn't come through the door or window. Almost all bars or other public places eventually had them.

GRUNT: Infantry, the backbone and the true strength of the US Marine Corps and Army. The Marine MOS for a (real) grunt is 0311. It is not wise to mess with grunts.

GUNG HO: The term is probably of Chinese origin. It means enthusiastic or dedicated. Generally it is a complementary term.

GUNGY: See **Gung ho**. This term is generally used sarcastically, but not always.

HATCH: Doorway or entry into a room or building. Ships always have a hatch and not doors. Those hatches are watertight when closed.

HE or HEs: "High" or "heavy explosives."

HEAD: Bathroom, restroom, or where ever it was that you went to go so you could go. Ya know?

HIGH ROAD: Generally meaning that we will be going out of our way to make enemy contact, even though it was possible that we could have avoided it.

HOOCH: It can be your rack in the comfort of the barracks or a tent or just a poncho. It could also be a cardboard box for that matter—just wherever you intend to go to sleep or rest. See also **Ten toes.**

HOUSE MOUSE: A private in boot camp that "volunteered" to care for a drill instructor's equipment or belongings. Although a dubious honor, it often would lead to a promotion at the end of boot camp.

HUEY: The UH-1 ("Utility helicopter 1", Iroquois helicopter, which was the main chopper used until the end of the war. It was produced from 1959 until 1962, when it was ultimately replaced with the UH-60 Blackhawk. The UH-1 was *officially* known in the Marine Corps as the *Huey,* never as the Iroquois.

HUNKER: To get down, lie, sit, squat.

HURT LOCKER: Not really a locker at all. The hurt locker was anything that has, did, or may cause you pain or discomfort. Getting cut by something will put you in a hurt locker for a while. The *big* hurt locker was the hospital.

HUSS: A favor or helping another person to make something easier or to ultimately go your way.

INCOMING: As opposed to *outgoing.* It is a huge difference! Incoming may be bullets, bombs, rockets, or artillery. Outgoing sounds good, incoming changes your present situation immensely.

INDIAN COUNTRY: The term comes from the Wild West. If the enemy controls the land, it is indeed, Indian country.

ITR: Infantry Training Regiment. This was an extension of boot camp for us in the old corps. We learned basic infantry skills and fired any weapon system that would conceivably be found at battalion level. *All* marines went to ITR in the "Old Corps."

INTEL: A shortened version of *intelligence.* Spooks are intelligence people, and please notice that I didn't say "intelligent," but "intelligence." I was the exception, of course.

LANCE CORPORAL: Marine enlisted ranks are in order as follows: Private (E-1); private first class, or PFC (E-2); lance corporal, or LCPL (E-3); corporal or CPL (E-4); sergeant, or SGT (E-5); staff sergeant, or SSGT (E-6); gunnery sergeant, or GYSGT (E-7); master or first sergeant, MSGT or 1stSgt (both E-8); master gunnery sergeant or sergeant major, MGSGT or SGTMAJ (both E-9).

LBGB: "Little bitty gook boat." Small craft used for fishing or transportation. Often an entire family made their home on them. Because there were thousands of these, it was natural that the enemy also used them to transport weapons, explosives, ammunition, etc.

LPH: "Landing platform helicopter." A ship that looks like a small aircraft carrier but only has helicopters and not airplanes. Some WWII ships were converted, but they have all been replaced with newer ships and redesignated as LHA, LHD, LPD, or LSD. These ships, with the marines aboard, are America's 911 response team also known as the Fleet Marine Force, or FMF.

LZ: "Landing zone." Hot LZs were under fire and avoided by all pilots except the exceptional men who would fly into hell to get us out. More than one Medal of Honor was won at LZs.

M-14: The 7.62-caliber rifle used in the Cold War and into Vietnam. It was replaced by the inferior .223-caliber M-16. The M-14 was a lethal and splendid rifle.

M-16: This .223 piece of shit caused a lot of marine and army men to *die*. It is this author's opinion that .22-caliber bullets are for hunting bunnies, squirrels, and other ("vicious") prey, not people. Nuff said!

M-60: A medium-weight 7.62-caliber machine gun introduced in 1957. It was the standard automatic weapon for all branches of the service and is still found in use some places. It served us quite well.

MA DUCE: The M-2, .50-caliber heavy machine gun, affectionately known as the "Ma Duce.". The M-2 has been in continuous use since 1920 and is in all probability is not replaceable!

MAE WEST: A personal flotation device, commonly called a "life jacket." It is designed to keep the wearer's face out of the water and pointed toward the sky. Pointing down would be considered unsatisfactory. It was (unofficially) named after the buxom actress, Mae West during WWII.

MEDAL OF HONOR: The Medal of Honor is the highest military decoration awarded by the United States of America. Since 1941, over one-half have been awarded posthumously. There are actually three different versions of the Medal of Honor. There is one for the navy and Marine Corps, a different one for the army, and still a different version for the Air Force. Erroneously called the "Congressional Medal of Honor," it is simply the Medal of Honor and the only decoration or medal to be worn around the neck.

MCRD: "Marine corps recruit depot." This is where boys and girls become Marine Corps men and women. One is located at San Diego, California, and the other one is at Parris Island, South Carolina. Being a drill instructor is, without a doubt, the *hardest* job in the Marine Corps, and they have to volunteer for the job too. My "Smokey Bear" hat is tipped to you incredible men and women. *Semper Fi!*

MILK RUN: A routine mission that should not involve combat. The term "piece of cake" and "cake walk" could also apply. This one still makes me smile.

MOS: "Military occupational specialty. It is simply a numerical designation to identify what your job is. An 03 is infantry, the 11 would indicate you are a basic rifleman, making you 0311. Another example would be 0341; while still 03, the 41 indicates that this person is a mortar man.

MPC: "Military payment certificate." This currency was also known as "funny money," "monopoly money," or just plain MPC. There were no coins—it was all paper. Greenback dollars were illegal to possess. They were small in size and strange colors. Old MPC would be turned in for new issue a couple of times a year.

NCOIC: "Noncommissioned officer in charge." The officer in charge is the OIC.

NFG: "No fucking good"—not functioning or working properly, so it was probably made by the low bidder … once again.

NVA: "North Vietnam Army." Most soldiers and officers were well trained, disciplined, educated, and loyal. The majority of their forces were drafted.

OOOOHRAH: The meaning of *Oooohrah* is, well, "Oooohrah"! When this sound rumbles from a marine, it sounds something like a growl that comes from down deep inside the body. When it comes from someone in the army, it sounds more like … "Here kitty, kitty, kitty!"

PX: Post exchange, aka the store. The place to go and buy pogey bait and gee-dunk, sweet water (after shave) smokes, etc.

PIASTER: The local monetary exchange in South Vietnam when I was there in 1966 was 118 Piasters for one dollar of MPC.

POGEY BAIT: Candy, soda pop, desserts, and ice cream.

POGUE: Someone that has a cushy job or has it easy.

PORT: Navy lingo for the left side. Starboard would then be the … other side? The bow is the front of the boat or ship, and the aft or stern, is … yup, you got it.

POS: "Piece of shit," like the M-16 rifle that was first issued.

POW: "Prisoner of war," the forgotten few. Our government finally got around to giving POWs a medal in 1985. It is retroactive to 1917, but it is *way* too far down on the seniority list. That is again the author's opinion, and still is *my* book! In this case, my opinion is outstanding and final.

PTSD: "Post-traumatic stress disorder." PTSD is a very real illness. You can get PTSD after living through or seeing a dangerous event such as a war, hurricane, fire, death, or a serious accident. It is not restricted to the military.

PUFF THE MAGIC DRAGON: Call sign "**Spooky**." An old WWII aircraft equipped with three Gatling Guns that each were capable of firing six thousand rounds of 7.62 ammunition per minute. I'm happy that it was on our side.

PUNJI: Sticks or stakes that were simple, but deadly. Generally they consisted of sharpened bamboo placed in a camouflaged hole. The sticks angled down so they would impale you as you instinctively pulled your foot or leg up. Much of the time the hollow bamboo sticks contained human feces and urine for an extra bonus.

RF-4: The Phantom jet was a long range, supersonic fighter/bomber. The *R* designation indicated that the primary role of the aircraft was reconnaissance. In this case, the nose of the aircraft would have up to five high-resolution cameras plus infrared imaging and side-looking airborne radar imaging. This gave the aircraft both day and night capability.

RACK: Your bed, no matter where you were or how you got a place to sleep. Marines may have … another version or use of this particular word. Maybe horns on a deer or elk? Anyway … nice rack you have there!

RAIN LOCKER: The rain locker would be the shower.

REMF: "Rear-echelon motherfucker." A REMF is any noncombatant that remained in the rear with the gear. Those of us that were in intelligence would have been an exception, of course.

REMINGTON: The Remington M-40 sniper rifle was first seen in Vietnam in 1966. It held five rounds of 30.06, or 7.62 ammo.

SALTY: Any marine or sailor who has been around and knows the drill (the best way or the easy way). When they offer advice to you, they become a "sea lawyer."

SCUTTLEBUTT: Navy slang for rumor or gossip. Back in the days of sailing ships, water was stored in a butt or cask. To open a butt was to scuttle it. Later on, a scuttlebutt became a drinking fountain where rumors and gossip still abound.

SEMPER FI: Short for "*Semper Fidelis*"— "Always Faithful."

SILVER BOX: A casket that was standardized during the war. A way home for heroes—each and every one of them.

SIX ACTUAL: The officer (himself or herself) who is assigned the particular call sign. The radio operator uses the call sign, but the six actual was his OIC. My real radio call sign was, in fact, Chime Whiskey.

SKINNY: The scoop or the word. "The word" was the official word, and the scoop was the unofficial word. But the skinny was sometimes written in stone, at which it becomes the "straight skinny."

SNOOP AND POOP: Sneaking and peering about. Generally this was done covertly.

SNUFFY: A boot or someone who is out of the loop.

SOS: "Shit on the shingle" is a marine breakfast staple. Basically, it could be compared to creamed, chipped beef, but only marine SOS is really different. I think it is delicious!

SPLIB: a splib was a black Marine. Again, it wasn't a racial thing, it was just a Vietnam thing, I guess. Used in a joking manner, it could also be fighting words. See also **Chuck.**

SPOOK: Anyone assigned to or working within the intelligence (**intel**) community.

SPOOKY: The call sign for "**Puff the Magic Dragon.**"

SQUAD: A regular grunt squad would consist of twelve or more marines. In a specialized unit the squad, may be more or less people.

STARBOARD: Navy jargon for the right side. And once again the other side would be what? I'm proud of you!

TAD: "Temporary additional duty." Working or serving in a job or position that is not your primary MOS.

TEN TOES: Going to sleep or just lying down.

TIGER PISS: Unsatisfactory beer that is warm and tasted like toe jam. By the way, no I never have!

TIGER STRIPES: A type of camouflaged pattern that was black and brown on a green background. This pattern belonged to the ARVN, but was worn by advisors and some special ops guys.

TRACERS: A projectile with a hollow base containing a pyrotechnic material, generally loaded into a magazine every forth or sixth round. They allow the shooter to see where the rounds are impacting. The US version of the tracer is red, while the Soviet and Chinese tracers are green.

VC: Viet Cong or The National Liberation Front soldiers. They were especially adept at guerilla warfare.

ZEROING: The application of the proper dope to a weapon so the bullet will impact exactly as aimed.

ZOOMIES: Marines that are part of one of the Marine Corps four air wings and not a ground pounder. Generally the term is reserved for a pilot and air crew.

782 GEAR: Personal issued field equipment. This would include your helmet, back pack, haversack, poncho, canteen, pistol/cartridge belt, etc. This equipment was also known as "duce gear."

.45: The 1911 A-1, semi auto, .45-caliber pistol. It came out before WWI, in 1911, and has been the standard-issue sidearm for marines since then. I personally like the .45 over the nine-millimeter cartridge, but make no mistake—the nine-millimeter killed a lot of people, just in WWII.

---

i Posthumous Medal of Honor recipient, February, 28, 1967, while serving with the Second Battalion, Third Marine Regiment in Quang Tri. PFC James Anderson Jr. was the first African American marine to be awarded the MOH. Semper Fi, my brother marine!

ii Staff Sergeant Peter Connor was posthumously awarded the Medal of Honor for combat action on February 25, 1966. Staff Sergeant Connor succumbed to his wounds on March 8, 1966. I had the distinct pleasure of serving with Peter in 1/5 and the Second Battalion, Third Marine Regiment. A better "Danny Boy" was never sung than by this Irishman.

iii Private First Class Ronald L. Coker was born on August 9, 1947, and enlisted in the US Marines in Denver, Colorado. Coker was killed in action while serving with 3/3 in Quang Tri on March 24, 1969. I am proud to have been a member of his Honor Guard in Alliance, Nebraska. PFC Coker was awarded the Medal of Honor posthumously. Semper Fi, marine!

iiii Colonel Jay Vargas was a lieutenant where his actions at *Dai Do* saw him awarded the Medal of Honor in 1970. Colonel Vargas was also awarded the Silver Star and Purple Heart for other action as a grunt.

I first met Lieutenant Vargas while we were both with 1/5 at Camp Pendleton. We later rotated to FMF PAC as 2/3. Lieutenant Vargas is an outstanding officer and one of the finest officers that the Marine Corps ever had. He is the real thing, I'm damn proud to salute you Colonel Vargas!

Chapter 1

"Good morning, Lieutenant. I'm Lance Corporal McMullin, Perry V., 1981844, and I'm reporting for duty in accordance with my orders, *sir*."

"Well, good morning to you also, Lance Corporal McMullin. I think that we sorta expected to see you here about two days ago … as I recall, that is."

"Well, yes, sir. You are in fact correct. It seems that I ended up getting here by way of Saigon instead of the direct flight to Da Nang that I was supposed to be on. I guess there was some big brass on board the aircraft that needed to have special concessions made for them, so we went to Saigon first. I had to catch a hop from point A to point B, but you were supposed to have been notified by the army people about that little change of plan, Lieutenant. I guess that didn't happen though. Go figure, huh?"

The lieutenant seemed to be quickly growing weary of our conversation as he began to shuffle the stack of papers in front of him. "I wouldn't sweat the small stuff, Lance Corporal. Shit runs downhill, and I am just a notch above you here in Vietnam. Not everything goes as planned in a war zone, and it is what it is, but we'll probably extend your tour by two days to make up the difference." At least he was smiling at his comment as he waved me away so that he could return to the stacks of papers on the desk in front of him.

With the exchange of this pleasantry, I began the process of checking into the US Marine Corps Third Platoon of the First Reconnaissance Battalion, Third Marine Division. This particular platoon was just being formed on March 15, 1965. At that time, it came under the command of in-country Special Operations and Captain Ronald Barber. This platoon was used, for the most part, for covert operations and was generally broken down to be deployed in several different locations at the same time. No one should have ever questioned who, what, when, where, why, or how we accomplished a mission. In fact, they should not even ask if we had even been out on a mission. If they did question anything, either they would be completely out of line or they'd be one of us. As the recon guys used to say, "I didn't see nuth'n, I didn't hear nuth'n, and I didn't do nuth'n, cause I weren't even there!"

I had just turned twenty years old just after my graduation from boot camp in August 1964 at MCRD, San Diego. My dad had been a navy pilot during WWII and Korea, so I guess the military life always seemed like the natural route for me to follow after high school. I'd almost considered becoming a navy squid, but to me the Marines always seemed to have their shit together just a little bit more than the US Navy. Besides, the Marine Corps dress blues were awesome, and I really didn't want to wear a Dixie cup on top of my head and bell-bottom trousers with thirteen buttons. Tradition is a great thing and the Corps is full of cool traditions, but what if ya had to pee really bad? Getting those thirteen buttons undone seemed totally unsat[3] to me.

After three weeks of advanced infantry training, and then

---

3 Unsatisfactory

another three weeks of communications school, I was ready to attend my two very long months of Vietnamese language school. That didn't make me a full-fledged linguist by any stretch of the imagination, but I could communicate in Vietnamese with some reasonable efficiency. "Hold your own" was the catchphrase that was often used at the school.

I'd never taken Spanish in high school because I always said that anyone who was living in America needed to speak English. I guess it was fair to say that, if I was going to be in Vietnam, I should at least try to speak a bit of Vietnamese. Besides, I wasn't asked if I wanted to go; I was told I would, in fact, go to language school, and I was told that I was going to learn!

I made private first class out of boot camp because I'd been a house mouse, but being either a private or private first class in the marines is a lot like being a mushroom—you are kept in the dark all the time, and some shit would be heaped on you a few times each day. Somehow, that was supposed to make you grow into something usable at some point and time. Indeed, we were all some very, very dangerous mushrooms too. Mushrooms that, if not properly respected, could cause you to wake up dead.

Eleanor Roosevelt once said, "The marines I have seen around the world have the cleanest bodies, the filthiest minds, the highest morale, and the lowest morals of any group of animals I have ever seen. Thank God for the United States Marine Corps."

There had been some brief discussion about my attending a formal sniper school at the Marine Corps Base in Quantico, Virginia. Instead of that, I was taught the very basics of sniping at the First Marine Division, Camp Pendleton, California. My MOS[4] was still that of a 0311, or basic grunt. Nevertheless, the prospects of serving with real recon marines were thrilling to me, to say the least. A real

---

4 Military occupational specialty

marine sniper would have had the MOS of 0317, but I knew that I'd get there in due time, and I really wanted that elite sniper job title and MOS.

Recon missions were quite a bit different from what the field grunts did on their search and destroy sweeps. Most grunts held down some shit-hole, nasty-ass firebase in the frigg'n armpit of Vietnam. This was a beautiful country, but the Marine Corps always seemed to seek the worst possible parts of the world for their bases to be built. It was said that, if God ever gave the world an enema, He would find the nearest US Marine Corps base so he'd know exactly where to stick the damn hose. Amen, sayth my brothers that simply exist out in the boonies.

It seemed that a regular, oh-three grunt was generally just another number to generals, colonels, and other high-ranking officers. It wasn't until you got down to your platoon or squad level that you actually became more than just another warm body dressed in Marine Corps green. Rank is sorta like the game of chess—if you are the pawn, you are dispensable, but if you rank higher, you may actually have a legitimate move on the great chessboard of life.

That's not to say that marines are like the army soldiers, because our officers care about their men and women. Marine colonels and generals don't get their bird or a star by becoming politically correct.

Recon specializes in small-unit operations most of the time, so I knew I'd be getting some quality trigger time while serving with these elites. Plus, my chances of getting a decent personal medal or decoration while with recon was a hell of a lot better than I'd ever see in a regular grunt outfit. War may not be all about decorations, but look at all of the medals that have been designed just for those with a big brass ass. There was no way in hell that the average jarhead snuffy would ever get one of those medals. They were created to be chest fluff for colonels, generals, or maybe a sergeant major, but not for us snuffies. I wanted something on my chest to show off after I'd done my thing in Vietnam, when I finally did go back to the real world again.

"Oooohrah! Semper Fi! Do or Die!"

I finished checking into my unit, which actually turned out to be a hell of a lot more expeditious than any other admin procedure was back stateside. I guess that my being in a real true-blue shooting war changed the way all the chickenshit paperwork was done back in the land of the round eyes and the big PX.

Even going over to supply and drawing my Remington sniper rifle was far more simplified.

"Okay, Lance Corporal, sign here for the rifle, sling, scope, and one hundred match-grade rounds to get your rifle sighted in. Oh, and uh, keep yerself off of the skyline out there, you boot-ass grunt."

What the hell? I thought. Even though I was still a newbie in country, I resented the shit out of this REMF[5] supply corporal, shooting his mouth off to me about staying off the frigg'n skyline. That basic knowledge stuff was taught to every marine in the ITR.[6] If the enemy can see you silhouetted with the sky behind you, they will have the easiest shot of their life and probably the last of yours. This is very basic knowledge and common sense if you want to survive in combat, so I couldn't resist my salty retort to this scurvy-ass, rear echelon, noncombatant, supply pogue: "Well, gee, thanks beaucoup for that super-critical information, Corporal. I'll just bet that you get shot at a lot here in this nasty ole supply hut, along with all of these other supply pogues, huh?"

He glared at me for a moment and then he smiled a big grin, showing a gold tooth in the very front of his mouth. He opened the

---

5 Rear-echelon motherfuckers
6 Infantry-training regiment

bottom half of the Dutch door and glared at me as he stepped out from behind it. "I'll give yer boot-ass another chance at life there, my chuck friend. I'm here in this nasty ole supply hut because I'm recuperating from a bullet wound that gave me my third—count em, recruit—that's ba[7] Purple Hearts. Right now, you need to shut your cracker-ass face and listen up to those that have already walked a mile through the valley of the shadow of death. I got hit a long time before yer shiny-ass boots ever even set foot in the dirt of this country. Now, if you want to go home alive after your tour of duty in 'Nam, you need to open up those li'l ol' bunny froo-froo ears and shut yer clap trap! Now then, you can say 'thank you' to me for setting yer slacker-ass straight. Any time you need to know the straight skinny about something, you can come and talk with this here splib, Corporal James Anderson Jr.[1] Remember who's on yer side there, lad, and knock that newfound chip of yours completely off your shoulder. You are still lower than whale shit, and that resides at the bottom of the ocean. Leave me nowww, and be cooool, my lil brotha from a different muthaaa!"

As I was walked out of the hatch,[8] I stopped and turned back to see the gold-toothed smile that was still there. I wanted to say thanks to him for a valuable lesson well-learned, but instead, I gave Corporal James Anderson Jr. a snappy salute before I did an about-face and double-timed back to my hooch.

I was now better versed in manners, knowledge, and protocol, and not nearly as quick to make unfounded judgment call. Salty marines like I'd just pretended to be can be desalinized very, very quickly in the Marine Corps. My lesson for today was not to assume, because it makes an ass of you and me.

*   *   *

---

7 Three
8 Door

I was super-hyped to get the word telling me when I could go to the rifle range to acquire the proper dope[9] to sight this brand-new Remington thirty-aught-six bad-boy in. Once I had fired the rifle and made the crosshair corrections dope, I'd be able to put a bullet on target from the thousand-yard line—no sweat, GI.

Anything that was five hundred meters or less was going to be like shooting the eye out of a gnat with this beautiful, customized weapon. Now, when you're talking about five hundred meters or more, this is where a sniper and a regular marine grunt parted company.

As riflemen, the regular marines qualify at the two, three, and five-hundred-yard lines. The M-14 rifle can make a thousand-meter kill-shot when it is in the right hands. However, this new plastic "Mattie Mattel" ArmaLite, or M-16 rifle, that was coming out soon, was a pitiful, frigg'n .22-caliber joke. The army was supposed to adopt this stupid pray and spray, pissy-ass, plastic POS,[10] but I was hoping the marines would not cave into the intense political pressure. It is one thing to go to war with something that you know was made by the low bidder but being a POS and being made by the low bidder was just insane!

*   *   *

I suppose that all of the shooting expertise I had demonstrated while at the rifle range during boot camp actually amounted to something here in the Green Machine.

Talk the talk and then strut the walk, Marine!

On my third day at Da Nang, I was getting extremely itchy to go over to the range and pop me some caps on my new rifle. I mean, what the hell? I am here to shoot things, so what seems to be the

---

[9] Crosshair corrections
[10] Piece of shit

massive holdup? I was ready to lock and load on full auto at any time or any day, now that I was in country.

You can either lead me or you can follow me, but you need to get the fuck out of my way, either way.

*   *   *

After morning chow, I beat feet over to the admin office one more time to see what was jacking up my whole range process. Go figure, the person I needed to see was out of the area for the rest of the damn day, so it was to be stand by to stand by once again. The new butter-bar lieutenant stood up and motioned for me to come over to him.

"Lance Corporal, this is our new navy corpsman, John Fox. He's just off the C-130,[11] so I need for you show him the ropes about getting his ass checked in and then find him a place to cop a squat in your hooch."

"Aye-aye, sir. Will do," I said while still trying to sound a bit salty and reasonably official.

"Oh, hey, by the way there, Lance Corporal, are you aware that you have a range time set for tomorrow from 0800 to 1100 hours? Take this FNG[12] swabbie along with you and teach him something about shooting. God knows that these squids don't know which end of a rifle they'd need to kill the enemy." It occurred to me that the lieutenant must have forgotten that marines are skilled in killing with either end of a rifle. It just depends on how far away from you the enemy is at the time. I suppressed my smile to a simple grin, thinking that the new lieutenant had a lot of nerve calling the corpsman an FNG. Where was Corporal Anderson when I wanted him?

Once again, I acknowledged with an "Aye, sir. Will do," as we boogied away from all the admin type of office pogue, REMFs sitting

---

[11] Military cargo and transport aircraft
[12] Fucking new guy

there on their flat asses, looking so all frigg'n fired, refined, and important in their newly issued and starched-up jungle fatigues.

"Hey, Doc, so you just got in country, to Vietnam?" I asked him. I didn't want to tell him that I'd just arrived a few days ago too—not just yet, anyway.

"Yeah," he said, "but I was told that I was going to be assigned to the base hospital or sickbay once I got here. What is up with this recon infantry outfit anyway? Somehow, I think it has something to do with my getting the big screw applied to me. I can just feel it coming somehow. BOHICA!"[13]

I filled Navy Corpsman Fox in on some things about the Marine Corps, and specifically about recon units. With him just getting out of medical school, he didn't know much about Marine Infantry Units, and, right now, that might go in his favor. If he was expecting to be assigned to the base hospital or sickbay, this was going to be much, much worse than he could imagine.

I tried to console him a little bit, though. "This may not be the gig you expected, Doc, but I'll tell you one thing for sure—recon marines are tight! They are so tight they're like a frog's ass, and that, my friend, would be watertight! Just go with the flow for a while, Doc, and, well, who knows where your little amphibious webbed feet might land you?"

Getting Doc Fox checked in was done in super-record-time, because he got most of his stuff from the navy and not the marines. Except for his navy dress uniform, he would wear the same one we wore when we were out in the bush. One thing no one wanted to do was to look different from the person who was next to you. That was exactly why the army medics and the navy corpsmen quit wearing the helmet with the red cross within the white circle after the Korean War—it made an excellent target. Radio operators also

---

[13] Bend over, here it comes again

hated the fifteen-foot antenna sticking up from their radio, but there wasn't any way of getting rid of that and keeping a functional radio. That's also why officers quit wearing their shiny-ass rank insignia—anything a grunt could do to look like the jarhead next to him was a good thing. It wasn't so much the bullet that supposedly had your name on it; it was all of the others that said "to whom it may concern."

"After we get your rack set up in my hooch, we'll stop by Lord and Taylor, and we'll get you a set of tiger-stripe utilities ordered up. The locals here can measure you today and bring your finished set in for you tomorrow. They'll be cheaper if you pay in our MPCs[14] than in piasters[15] like you're supposed to. If you have any stateside greenbacks on you, Doc, you'll need to get them converted into the Monopoly money."[16]

Military money looked strikingly like Monopoly money in its simplicity and color. Why it was named military payment certificates instead of the obvious military money was to me just another secret acronym mystery.

John looked at me and said, "Lord and Taylor is here, on this base? Really, Lord and Taylor is here in Vietnam?"

How could I resist his wide-eyed amazement? I laughed at John, because he fell for the joke the same way I had, and the same way every other new guy does. "Well, the people that make them are tailors, and you just hope to the good Lord that they will be big enough to fit you. It's an inside joke, John. I'm sure you'll get someone with the same one, like I just did you. We pretty much have to make our own humor at times while in country.

"And, by the way, Doc, when we go to the marine supply hut, I want to introduce you to Corporal James Anderson Jr. He is

---

14 Military payment certificates
15 The local monetary exchange in South Vietnam.
16 MPC

on his third Purple Heart for this tour, and he still refuses to go home. A cool guy; not humble at all, but a cool splib, through and through."

Corporal Anderson was no longer working in supply, the sergeant said. "He just couldn't stand being stuck behind a desk anymore so he actually extended his enlistment and went back to 2/3,[17] That's his old unit that is up somewhere near Cam Lo. I think he may be nuts, but then I strongly suspect that all of you grunts are genuinely certifiable nut cases."

Tiger-stripe cammies were not issued to US troops, but the advisors and some South Vietnamese Army units had worn them for years. They were a hell of a lot more effective than the crummy plain-green jungle fatigues that were being issued by our supply, because these actually allowed you to blend into the jungle. The Vietnamese soldiers were light years ahead of the US Soldiers who were still wearing WWII uniforms and using much of the same equipment that was issued during the last two wars.

I don't think that the regular marines could wear the tiger stripes, but if we paid for them out of our own pocket, no one said anything about our owning or wearing them.

"Speaking of tigers, Doc, after we get you checked, in we'll go over to the E-club, and each of us will have a big ol' pitcher of tiger piss. Some people would call it beer, but I think you'll agree it really is more like tiger piss once that nasty, warm liquid hits your lips."

We sat under a tarp to keep the hot July sun off of us as we drank one and then another pitcher of something that was at very best, just *am ap va mau vang.*[18]

In just two hours of ratchet-jawing we knew just about everything that was worth telling the other person about ourselves—who, what,

17 Second Battalion, Third Marine Regiment
18 Warm and yellow

when, why, and how; born, raised, parents, brothers and sisters, girlfriends, school, and now here.

And we also confirmed that there actually are tigers in Vietnam. The salty grunts always talked about soldiers being dragged off in their sleeping bags while asleep, but they spoke of the tigers like they were vampires, or something to that effect. Half of the stories told by the salty guys were pure bullshit, and the other half was somewhere close to it.

Chapter 2

John thought that the title of Doc was an honor that was premature, with his having just completing corpsman school. I assured him that, in the Marine Corps, every corpsman was called Doc. When he joined the navy, he said that he wanted to become an assistant to a chaplain, but the needs of the military often lead us in a different direction. If whatever the recruiter told you wasn't put into writing, then it didn't exist later on and, apparently, that applied to all branches of the services the same exact way.

In the 'Nam, our real names were seldom, if ever, used. Everyone acquired a nickname, or a tag name, as it were. That was who you'd be until the day you rotated back to the land of the big PX. Because I was still an FNG myself, I wouldn't get tagged until the salty recon guys came back from the field. It was too damn lame to pick your own tag name, and it was doubtful that it would ever be used if you did.

*   *   *

For the time being, we were the only two in the hooch for four people, because the other two salty marines were out there someplace, beating the bush. It was somewhere near—oh dark thirty—when the two of them came rolling into the tent, stinking of mud, sweat, and, in general, just the way the unwashed human body smells from the earth. Of course, they immediately turned on the light and went crashing about like two bulls in a frigg'n china shop as they quickly stowed their gear away.

Doc and I introduced ourselves and asked to hear the scoop regarding their mission, but it was obvious that this wasn't going to be discussed. Our newbie status was obvious.

"Okay, you two buttheads, listen up. If you weren't with us, then you don't have the need to know diddley shit about where we were and what we did."

That said, Animal introduced himself, and then Crooner added, "Besides, if we told you two shit-maggots anything, then we'd just have to kill you. Then, if we were to kill you both tonight, all you'd have on your chest was your chicken-shit fire watch[19] ribbon when they sent your scroungy, stinking-ass body back home to yo mama.

"Right now, you two aren't even cleared for scuttlebutt[20] from the head, so after you both get some time in Vietnam, even you two bastards can act salty. Factually, that time ain't here yet, though."

They shed their rancid tiger stripes and headed off to the rain locker[21] to shower off the accumulated crud from their bare-ass bodies—well, naked that is, except for their flip-flops.

Animal had apparently obtained his tag during his last liberty while in Oceanside, California, just ten days before deploying to Vietnam. The story I heard was that he had thrown another marine off of the Oceanside pier and into the frigid ocean below. I guess they'd been drinking at a nearby beach party, and the other marine said something rude and crude about Animal's girlfriend—like she

19 National-defense
20 Rumors
21 Shower

had loose morals, or something to that effect. Animal wasn't just content with the thirty-foot fall into the ocean, he began tearing off anything he could get his hands on and throwing it at the floundering man as he was trying desperately to stay afloat. Apparently, when the Oceanside police finally arrived, Animal tried to toss both of them over the side too.

He was let out of jail early so he could deploy to Vietnam, or he would have had done at least thirty days behind bars. Like he said, "They could keep me in jail with three hots and a cot or shave my head and send me to Vietnam. I didn't get to vote on the decision, though, and jail was outstanding compared to doing the year here."

Crooner got his tag because he'd had a fledgling singing career before he'd become a marine. The word was that he sounded a lot like Ol' Blue Eyes himself, and he even made a record that had done pretty well after it hit the market.

I guess that wanting to be a marine isn't just limited to those of us with no real talent. Someday, it would be cool to say I knew the Crooner Jones when he was just another grunt like me.

When you finally came out of the boonies, a hot shower was generally priority number one. Number two was some hot chow and cold milk—chocolate if they had any. Number three was a trip into that shithole village for some stateside beer and this hour's newest lust of your life. Hopefully she'd either be on top or underneath you for the next hour or so. All of that would cost you maybe fifteen bucks in MPC—that is if you negotiated while you were still sober. When you are all jacked up on alcohol, you'd always find that thinking with the little head will send you back to camp limping like some poor ol' broke-dick dog!

It was a strange phenomenon that we could only get warm *ba moi ba*[22] beer at the E-club, but somehow there was always plenty

---

22 Thirty-three

of stateside beer available out there in the *ville*. It was just like we couldn't get some things issued to us at our own supply warehouse, but things could be obtained on the black market out there in the village. If you had the money needed, you could buy damn near anything, up to and including a brand new AK-47 rifle, in the village. It was amazing that things were never in stock at supply, but it was for sale in the *ville*.

Someone besides President Johnson was getting very, very rich from this war.

At 0700 that morning, Fox and I got some chow and then we headed over to the rifle range.

We both decided that marine cooks must be highly trained to be able to take the same food the army, navy, and air force got and turned it into something that resembles dog food from a can. After a while, you quit asking what it was and you just ate it. The one good thing we got at morning chow was SOS, or shit on the shingle. That was probably a recipe that was handed down the day the United States Marine Corps was formed, on November 10, 1775, at Tun Tavern, Philadelphia, Pennsylvania.

I brought along an extra hundred rounds of match ammo that I'd acquired while out in town, so, after zeroing in my rifle, Doc could get himself some trigger time in also. There is a big difference in the accuracy of factory-loaded ammo and match grade. Each match-grade round was individually hand-loaded and inspected. An inch either way could mean a hit or a miss.

They didn't get to shoot very much in navy boot camp, but if Fox was going to be a corpsman within a recon outfit, he'd have to learn to fire every stinking-ass weapons system that we could even remotely come in contact with. That included all of the stuff the VC and NVA carried also. By the time we left the range at twelve hundred, Doc was already one damn good spotter and a fair five-hundred-yard shot with my sniper rifle.

We would both spend the whole next week shooting and blowing up all sorts of things with any kind of explosive that became available to us. It was cool to have that much fun and still be paid for it.

Doc fired the 3.5 rocket launcher, RPG, flamethrower, M-1 and M-14 rifles, the M-79 grenade launcher, the M-60 machine gun, the Soviet-made AK-47 and SKS rifles, along with the eighty-one- and sixty-millimeter mortar. Then came the 1911A1 .45 pistol, 1921A Thompson submachine gun, the BAR[23]) and the "Ma Duce" fifty-caliber machine gun. After throwing a half dozen or more Mark-24 hand grenades and a few lessons with his KA-Bar knife, he was getting closer to being a real US Marine Corpsman.

Even Doc was saying "Oooohrah" now, and he was starting to like this gig a little better than being stuck with a bunch of uptight and outta sight officers at the hospital. He was even coming up with classic marine terms like *Gung ho, Semper Fi, lock-and-load*; 782 gear, and "the more you sweat in peace, the less you bleed in war." This was unique Marine Corps lingo that the navy guys didn't know.

The thing I wanted most to pass along to this squid friend of mine was what our drill instructors beat into our gourds us at least ten frigg'n times a day: "The United States Marine Corps is now your family. The Corps is yer mama, yer daddy, yer sister, yer brother, and that scroungy, unfaithful skirt you left behind you.

"You will live and breathe: *Unit … Corps … God … Country*! Marines always have, and always will: live, breathe, serve, and die, and in that order only!

"There is only room in your life for one other thing, and that is optional once you wear the eagle, globe, and anchor of a United States Marine! Remember, if the Marine Corps wanted you to have a wife, they would have issued you one."

---

23 Browning automatic rifle

It all sounded a bit hokey to me at first, but before I graduated from boot camp, we each knew this was what separated US Marines from the rest of the world—attitude ... pure, unadulterated *attitude*!

*   *   *

Both Animal and Crooner were now super salty corporals, as they were officially short timers. This put them into the category that fell into the "Fuck it, I've got my orders," or FIGMO as we knew it. It was their time to rotate stateside on the big freedom bird[24] that would take you back stateside. When you got short, they generally tried to cut you a huss by not sending you out on the really dangerous missions. This allowed the salty guys to spend beaucoup time teaching us boots the fine art of snooping and pooping while out in the bush. Being FIGMO was a big deal to everyone, even to the officers.

At least two hours a day were now being spent on the rifle range, with us firing the Remington BDL and the M-14 rifle. Doc Fox definitely was becoming the best spotter a shooter could have, but Doc wasn't just about the shooting either; he could pick up a one-to-fifty-thousand map and a lensatic compass and throw you back a magnetic azimuth faster than any marine I ever knew.

Later in the week, Animal and Crooner came strutting their shit into the hooch after they had picked up their orders to return stateside. Animal had this huge, shit-eating grin on his face, like something was up, and he was simply busting a gut to tell us about it.

"The time has come for us to pack our sea bags and to go back to the real world, the land of the big PX, the land of the round eyes, the nest of the freedom bird and the state side hamburger stand. Crooner then jumped right in with, "Yeah, but you two shit-eating

---

[24] Airplane

maggots won't be here to carry our stuff for us because you'll both leave at 0530 tomorrow for a full week of survival school. Now isn't that a damn shame, Animal, because we have to hump those heavy old sea bags all by ourselves."

Animal had copped a squat on his rack, sorting through the clothing he would take home with him and things he would leave behind. "Doc, I know you have never done anything that even remotely resembles survival school, so welcome to the real Marine Corps. You will be eating and drinking things you never even dreamed were edible in just a few days. How about you, McMullin, did you ever do any real survival training?"

"Nope, not really, Crooner," I told him. "All I have done was just the overnight thing we do in infantry training after boot camp. I guess it is mandatory training for us here, before we can go out into the bush alone, huh?"

Crooner was grinning from ear to ear as he spouted off, "Oh, you two will love it, because it is seven glorious days of being pampered in a luxury hotel setting, with three gourmet meals served to you each day. Really, guys, what's not to love and to cherish about survival training? Ain't that right, Animal?"

These two assholes were in hog-slop heaven while they were pimping us about the rigors of this grueling training.

"The best part comes after you have just spent two days in that open air classroom that's just swarming with blood thirsty *muoi*,"[25] Animal said. "When you get captured, and trust me, you will; well, that's when the fun really gets started. The guys acting like the enemy were actually the real thing just a few weeks ago, but they switched sides for the money we pay them. Don't think for one second that they like you any better, because they don't. They can abuse ye ass and get paid for it, but you can't shoot them. If we just

---

[25] Mosquitoes

put the entire enemy on the US payroll, we could all go home and become civilians again, and there'd be no war here. "

Now Crooner had to put his two-cents worth in once again. "You stay in the POW camp for three very ugly nights with little or no sleep. Then they sorta arrange for you to escape. You'll live off of the land, with absolutely nothing to work with but your mind and your hands. During the two nights you are in the bush, you are on your own, and you'll have to make your way back to the base camp. By the way, the bad guys will be hunting you, and if you get captured again, you'll start the training phase all over. At that point, you will have only had one sticky-rice ball, complete with weevils, to eat. I hope you two like to eat all sorts of bugs, worms, snakes, and drinking tree bark tea. The grub worms are pretty tasty if you can fry them—which you won't be able to do!" This comment evoked little-girl giggles and a high five from these two crusty warriors. That was something of a contrast for them and maybe symbolic of what a year in country would do to a person's mind.

Animal mouthed back with, "Just remember this while you are out there—pain is just weakness leaving your body, and pain is also just a temporary inconvenience. That is, unless you get captured for real by the bad guys, and then you're just dead meat, because they don't keep American enlisted men as POWs. Think about that li'l fact for a moment; how many of the known POWs are enlisted and how many are officers? You don't want to get captured, trust me."

Later in the evening, Animal and Crooner were ready to leave for the out-processing barracks to catch an early flight home. This one time they both actually seemed to be almost civil in their conversation to John and myself. They shook our hands and wished us well during the remainder of our tour. Once again, they warned us not to become too close with others.

"If or when they get killed, you will take it personally, if they were your friends."

"You are both pretty squared away, so stay the hell off of the skyline and remember—no strange pussy for at least one month prior to your rotation."

They had each piled up various items they were leaving behind on our racks. Crooner smiled as he said, "There isn't much need for old duce gear back stateside and since both of us will be getting out in less than six months, we thought you guys would have super-fond memories of us with some of our salty things." With that said, they both disappeared into the inky darkness of the nightly imposed camp blackout.

Survival training was indeed pretty tough going, but knowledge was passed on that was going to possibly save our lives, over and over. We were now on our own for training purposes and not teamed together with anyone. That really made it harder, because all you could do was talk to yourself, and you couldn't disagree with the last decision that you just made.

The black-pajama gang got a reward of extra food if they caught you and returned you to the POW camp, so they were as motivated as we were to not being captured. The thing is that they had done this for real, and they also knew the lay of the land because they did this full time. The more real the training, the more real your chances of survival became, I guessed. Both John and I managed to avoid capture, and I made it back a full twelve hours before he did. Still, that was pretty darned impressive for a squid, corpsman or not. He came in ahead of several marines, no matter how you look at it.

It was amazing the things a person could eat and drink to stay alive when McDonald's, Taco Bell and 7-11 had already closed for the night. Fast food takes on a new meaning when you pick it up off of the ground and eat it while running as fast as you can.

*   *   *

When we returned from survival training, we met up with Staff Sergeant Larry O'Donnell. He was to be our link to staying alive in a combat zone, as he was now our new NCOIC[26] of training. This was the man who would teach us the real way to survive in a place where just 148 grains of an FMJ[27] bullet would end your young-ass life and send you home in the box.

All of your phony stateside high school friends would try hard to say nice things about you that they never bothered to say to you when you were still alive. How sweet it is that some sweet skirt[28] from high school will only remember and praise you once you are dead. Neither she, nor any other of your former classmates, could have given you a rigid, royal-ass up yer's, nor would they have even remembered your name a few months ago. So it is, and so it shall be, I guess.

---

[26] Noncommissioned officer in charge
[27] Full metal jacket
[28] Girl

Chapter 3

As we began to enter the real world of kill or be killed, we also became subjected to the reality of combat. It was time that Doc and I were assigned to a squad that was mostly just for all of the administrative bullshit. Our squad leader was Sergeant Joe Morley, a lifer who hailed from Hartford, Connecticut. Now, he and Staff Sergeant O'Donnell were real Marine Corps marines! These two guys weren't just gungy; they were truly out there to train you and to see that you got home alive—and walking tall. They didn't just feed you a bunch of Marine Corps handbook crap; they really cared about each and every marine with whom they came in contact.

Spending time with Sergeants Morley and O'Donnell is what made me actually decide to become a career marine. These two epitomized all that we were taught about in boot camp, and they became our mentors who told it like it really was out there in the real combat world.

A favorite saying from O'Donnell was, "To finish second in a gunfight is totally unsatisfactory marine behavior, and that alone will ultimately become grounds for future disciplinary action."

After we had been in country almost three weeks, we got to go out on some "minor" missions with either the recon marines, or in support of grunt operations. For the most part, we had it easy on the first three outings that we were on, and we were able to gain some much needed knowledge and confidence in our own abilities.

And then, on the fourth mission, the shit hit the fan, as we knew it ultimately was going to.

We had set up a covert location near a US fire base, along with another two-man sniper team. The marines here were getting random hostile fire on a regular basis from the hills around the camp. We deployed before daybreak to lay low and try to zap the enemy shooters on this particular morning.

This was our first real mission totally on our own, and it was a bit uneasy to be out there in the boonies with the enemy creeping around, hunting us also. The training stuff had pretty much ended for us, and this was, in all probability, going be our baptism by fire—no more training exercises, no one telling you that you screwed up, and either you or your partner would be dead because of any mistake you made. This was real, the enemy was real, and they used real bullets that would change or end a life. It was exciting, though, and this was what we'd prepared for, but I questioned if I had trained and listened well enough.

At first light, the enemy started with sporadic sniping at the camp, taking pot shots at anybody that showed themselves as targets. Generally, within the first couple of minutes, the enemy could inflict one or more killed or wounded before the marines could hunker down.

We watched intently to pinpoint the location of a couple of the shooters across the valley from us. One of the NVA or VC shooters wasn't even remotely camouflaged and he quickly became an easy kill shot for me at just six hundred and fifty meters. When I popped the cap in him, I got a nice warm feeling oozing all through me. It was sorta like how my first shot of whiskey went down and hit my stomach, hot and different somehow. I knew when I saw him slump down that he'd never jack up another marine, and that was what I was here for.

As soon as I fired, we picked up and scurried off to another location. But we remained alert to keep an eye open for the other shooters that we knew were still lurking out there.

I quickly picked up another scruffy-ass enemy soldier in my rifle scope while he was looking all around for us where we had just been. Didn't anyone bother to teach these dumbass bastards to move after each shot? This guy should have been an easy kill at just under six hundred meters, but I *missed* him by a full yard. It is so true; you have to squeeze the trigger and not jerk it, and I had just jerked the hell out of it. Damn, that pissed me the fuck off. If I hadn't been so frigg'n eager to up my body count … That was a gimme shot, and I blew it! This was an amateur mistake for real, and I knew that I'd not hear the end of it until I redeemed myself.

These guys out here had to be Vietcong, because the regular army was much better disciplined than this, from what we had been told. Maybe they thought this was easy for them, because they had pretty much gone unopposed for too long. At any rate, they were careless, and careless makes you finish in second place.

We were just set to move again when the air around us came roaring to life with one or more AK-47s blasting the shit out of our entire area. All we could do at that point was to try and bury our sorry asses in the dirt and become as small and as invisible as we possibly could, given the circumstances.

The Remington was pretty useless to us at the moment, so I grabbed the M-14 rifle in hope that someone would show themselves to me. I was peering off in the direction of the AK that was blasting away at us when I heard, *Bam! Bam! Bam!*

John had just let loose three quick rounds from his .45 pistol.

One of those assholes had crept right up on top of us before Doc saw him and smoked his ass. We would have become statistics for their side, right off, if Doc hadn't been right on top of things. I don't think that the dink actually knew for sure where we were, but he got lucky (or unlucky, as the case may be) this time around. Doc said that the VC had seen us just a fraction of a second before the three .45 caliber bullets impacted him square in his chest.

Just about then, another VC popped his slimy gourd (head) up to see where we were and who in the hell was shooting at whom. That mistake provided me an excellent chance to give him a sweet-ass 7.62 kiss right between his running lights.[29]

A bullet from a high-powered rifle such as the M-14 doesn't leave much of a head to identify someone by, and the magazine of twenty rounds insured that one of the three I'd just fired would take care of the job at hand. If there were any other enemy troops around us at that moment, they chose to boogie off rather than to stay around and probably die today also.

As we began to crawl away from the dead man, I couldn't resist, and so I leaned close to him and whispered, *Neu ban chay tu mot bien sniper ban se chi chet met moi asshole. Key hoi pnieu cua ma cho su than khoa tuoa tuong lai.*[30]

It seemed like we low-crawled about ten frick'n miles to get some distance between where we had just been burned[31] and our close call with death.

As we got closer to our firebase, we were challenged by two grunts located in an LP[32] just outside of the wire.

"Possible," came the low whisper from the unseen marine.

"Prudent," I whispered the counter sign back to the air around us.

---

[29] Eyes

[30] "If you try to run from a Marine Corps sniper, you will just die tired, asshole, so make a note of that for future reference."

[31] Discovered

[32] Listening Post

"Advance toward my voice and then wait for the word," the marine grunted back.

The Vietnamese had a real problem pronouncing *P*s, so we used that letter of the alphabet quite often. Indeed, that meant that when they tried to pronounce my first name, it came out *fairy* instead of *Perry*. I didn't like being called a fairy, but then I supposed I called them something a lot worse most of the time.

We lay there, searching, but we were unable to see the occupied LP because it was so well camouflaged. "Okay, you two, stay low and move on up toward the wire," the faceless voice said.

We crawled forward a skosh and, just as we reached the wire, a smiling, camo-painted, marine face popped up smack dab in front of us. "This way to Camelot, my friends. Just watch out for trip wires, punji sticks, naked whores, and a few claymore mines." I don't know about Fox, but I had to pee anyway, and that buzzard-bait bastard just about put me over the edge when he pulled that trick off.

We were then ushered into a bunker to get some rest and to chow down on some C-rats.[33] We both were given B-1s without even asking or choosing, and that was the grunts' way of showing us their appreciation. We could have been given B-2s or B-3s, because everyone knew the B-1s had fruit and a better meat choice, so the honor was there, just unspoken. God forbid we would have been given B-2s with ham and lima beans or we would have been farting up a storm the rest of the day. These C-rations were a rite of passage that had served the troops in WWII, Korea, and now in Vietnam. With some Tabasco Sauce and marine creativeness, some of them were almost tasty, considering we were eating meals that had been made in 1947.

After the survival training thing we had gone through, I couldn't

[33] C-rations

imagine ever bitching about eating anything that came in a jar or can again. The "pop" of a big white grub worm in your mouth is a life-lasting memory.

Chapter 4

"Perry, I want to ask you something before the other team arrives." I could see the look of obvious consternation on John's green-black-and-brown-painted face.

"Okay Doc, what's bothering you? Something sure seems to be stuck in your craw."

He was looking past me toward a tattered NVA flag that was hanging on the bulkhead of the bunker.

"That's the first time I've killed another person, and I'm not feeling very good about it. I mean, I know it's a war and all, but I could see the look on his face when those bullets hit his chest. It was like it all transpired in slow motion or something as I watched him die."

I said, "Come on, bro, it was him or us. He would have shot or bayoneted us for cry'n out loud. He didn't come over to visit or have a spot of tea; so what more is there to think about?"

John just looked at his C-rations, which were now burning on his homemade stove, and he let go a long sigh. "But I saw his eyes. It was like the life went out of him before he even fell. I saw his eyes as they went lifeless and then he nearly fell on top of me. I am a corpsman for cripes sake Perry; I'm supposed to be saving lives not taking them."

We both sat there in overwhelming silence for what seemed like a two hundred second minute. "Doc, that guy would have killed both of us back there and you damn well know that. You saved both of our necks because he was our enemy and it was kill or be killed. Personally, I'd rather it was his stinking, slant-eyed life that was snuffed out, rather than ours."

Fox was still staring at his chow that was now smoking like a frigg'n house that was on fire. "You make it sound so easy to take another person's life, Perry. Doesn't it bother you at all to have just shot and killed someone back there? I know I did what I had to do, but I'm still not feeling right about doing it."

I thought through what he had just said and I knew that I was no closer to convincing him now than I was a minute ago. "*Thanh cut.*[34] Fox, we are at war. We didn't come here to frigg'n slow dance with these bastards. After you kill the first one, they say it becomes easier, and I didn't find it all that bad when I capped off the first one back there. I can't think about it, Doc, and you *can't* either. It's something you just have to shake off, or it'll make you into a certified nutcase. Let it go, my brother; and besides, you may get yourself a medal for killing him."

That created an instant eruption from John as he kicked his now-charred food toward the door. "Oh, well, thanks a lot for that information, Perry. We'll both get nice little colored ribbon for hunting and killing another human being? That's outstanding; out-frigg'n-standing!"

I sorta had the idea of where he was coming from, but I was getting a little pissed with all of this feeling-sorry crap for that dead enemy soldier back there. "Come on, Doc, *let it fucking go*! We are supposed to be warriors and not some kind of missionaries. Leave it right here in this bunker before it'll consume you. So what, you saw his face when you killed him. BFD, Doc; big fucking deal!

---

[34] "Holy shit"

"I see every one of their faces up close and personal when I cap them, and that's just what I do as a sniper. Do you know what I feel for them, Doc? The only thing I should ever, ever feel is the recoil of my rifle. In each and every case, it is either him or me. Do you really think for one second that the slant-eyed fuck would be sitting there with second thoughts about our sorry asses if he would have killed us? He'd be stringing up your ears, right alongside mine, and then he'd probably be jerking off on them.

"You don't have to like this war or the killing, Doc, but if it bothers you so damn, then you should put in for a transfer—maybe transfer to the base hospital where you could see what they do to our marines and soldiers when they get killed. You'll see dead marines with their dicks and their ears cut off and kept as trophies by those yellow skinned bastards."

What else was there for me to say? Doc had a bug up his ass, and it wasn't coming out soon, if ever at all. He wouldn't be the first man to break after taking the life of another person—enemy or not.

"All right, look, Doc. We'll both just go and get totally obliterated when we get back. That will help us to blur, so you can just stuff all of those bad feelings away nice and tidy. It will be better in the morning, trust me on that. A bottle of Jack Daniels fixes most everything up, primo. In fact, think of it as being sort of medicinal, Doc."

It was his job to support us in the field, but he didn't have to tag along with me as a spotter. It was complex as hell, and neither of us had the answer as to why he did what he did. Maybe a lot of different reasons that would have never have made any sense back in the States.

*   *   *

A while later, Fox and I came in out of the field looking and feeling like we'd just been ridden hard and put away wet. It was only a three-day, two-night snoop-and-poop mission, but it rained from the time we left until the time we got back. We both knew what the expression "Cold to the bone" meant, because we both felt like our core temperature had fallen off to zero. All we wanted to do was to hit a hot shower and get some decent chow.

"Hey, Fox and McMullin! The old man[35] wants to see both of you at the company office before you shower and make chow. What'd you two guys do now?"

John and I looked at each other like we each ought to know something that the other one of us had held out from telling the other one about. We each then shrugged our shoulders and begrudgingly sauntered off toward the admin office.

"Jeez, I'm sure we both must stink like outhouse full of turds, John." I grinned. "I bet they'll be sorry they didn't let us hit the head and the rain locker first."

We walked inside the admin Quonset hut, and everyone instantly turned to see what had just come in and turned the air blue. I pointed my thumb at Fox and smirked as I said, "I think he may have just farted. Excuse yourself Corpsman Fox, cause you're *chi kho chiu!*"[36]

The captain handed each of us our unexpected promotion warrants and said, "You can now address Doc as Petty Officer Corporal McMullin, and Doc, you can now address your partner in crime as Corporal. Now then, nothing personal, but you two are seriously stinking up my office. Come back tomorrow with the cigars, and I'll do something more appropriate regarding your promotions. How appropriate depends on the quality of the stogies you bring along with you, however."

We were both pooped out after hitting the head for a hot shower,

---

[35] Commanding officer
[36] "Just nasty."

but nothing would do but for us to go to the NCO[37] club and buy many, many pitchers of beer to wet down our new stripes.

*   *   *

I had a spotter that was supposedly assigned to me, but he was always more than happy to stay back with the REMFs whenever he could. He wasn't recon trained either, and his lack of aggressiveness earned him the tag name of "Snatch," because calling him a pussy was just too blatant.

How he ever made it through boot camp was a wonder to me, but the Corps had accepted draftees for the first time since WWII, and he was one of them. Being drafted into the marines didn't work any better than throwing a cat into a lake just to see if he could swim. Sure, the cat, in all probability, would survive, but you still didn't make him into a swimmer that would want to go swimming on his own again.

Marines become marines because they possess something different within themselves, and they have persevered through wars and combat since 1775. The Corps had real, true-blue marines but there were also a few pogey, bait-eating, army-dropout, wannabe jarheads. Snatch was *E*—all the above!

---

37 Noncommissioned officer

Chapter 5

I was ordered to take Snatch along with me as my spotter, because he was just hanging around and getting on everyone's nerves at the complex. Doc was attending a four-day training thingy at the hospital to keep up to date on new technology regarding sucking chest wounds and on new equipment that was becoming available in the field.

We would be going into an area that had been receiving a significant number of enemy sniper events. A counter-sniper team was going to preposition themselves where they could observe myself and Snatch, plus observe the surrounding mountain, should the enemy sniper think we were easy prey. We had a plan in place that would make it appear that we were some kind of an amateur or rookie team that was out there looking for some something simple.

As the enemy sniper settled in for his easy target, he would hopefully become careless or make some kind of fatal mistake. At any rate, we were not going to be as simple to take out as we were allowing it to appear. We just wanted to look like newbies that were careless.

This team was supposed to be the best of the best, and everyone had pure-ass faith that it was these two professionals that would take the lesson home to the enemy. We were bait, pure and simple.

The counter-sniper team was already in place from the night before when we moved into our preset position, just prior to first light. I was not aware of their location, nor was that important to me, but what was important was that we would accomplish our mission without any actual injury to ourselves.

Snatch wasn't aware of the nature of our mission as bait, so I had to keep him from becoming an easy target due to his own stupidity. He had only been in the bush twice before and therefore our clumsy setup would not seem obvious to him. He might actually take some exception to our being used the way we were, however. In his case, ignorance remained bliss.

My lightly camouflaged rifle was left partially out in the open, as was my steel pot helmet that I never wore in the field—or even took along with me, for that matter. I was providing a textbook chapter on what not to do. I was going to see to it that both of us would remain low enough to have any round fired at us pass slightly over our bodies. Every minute or so, I would reach up and move my Remington or my brain bucket[38] to make it appear that only our very dimmest mental lights were on. The fact was, we wanted it to appear as if we were not paying attention to details.

Our situation was intense to the point that even I was jittery about being such an obvious target. Snatch seemed to think that we were on an outing of sorts however. As we laid, there hunkered down, the idiot next to me decided that he wanted to shoot the shit. "What's your name, Corporal? Mine is Edward, but all of my friends call me Eddy. You can call me Eddy if you want to."

I could not believe what I was hearing, and his attempt at a whisper sounded like thunder. I looked at him in disbelief and held my finger to my lips to get this moron to shut up. As I reached up

---

38 Helmet

to move my rifle, he started in once again as if my crusty look that I had just issued to him was unnoticed.

As his lips began passing gas again, I said, "If you don't shut the fuck up I'm going to change your name from Eddy to 'Deceased.' Now zip it!" Eddy remained sullen for the rest of the mission.

If nothing went down, we would remain in our position until the cover of darkness allowed us to make a safe retrograde and head for home. In that case the counter-sniper team would continue their observation and cover our six[39] as we pulled out.

At 1611, a glint of light crossed my rifle. I cautiously peered over the protective embankment, keeping my head a safe distance from my rifle and helmet. There was the mirror flash again, and it was the signal ID that was being used by our own friendlies, so I knew that something was up.

About a half-hour later, a voice whispered from behind us. "Corporal, pull out of there and move back toward the sound of my voice." That scared the shit out of Snatch and me both, because we had no idea that someone had come creeping up on our six o'clock and gotten so damned close to us.

We gathered up our things and began to crawl backward toward the vicinity of the voice.

"Stop, I'm over here," the voice commanded.

I saw a twig purposely wiggle, indicating the other marine's location. Talk about humility. I thought I was pretty good at camouflage until I saw this guy. He made me look like I just flunked Camo 101.

When we were actually able to eyeball each other, the counter-sniper handed me a note and signaled for us to follow him. I quickly glanced at it: "We got the sniper alive. U X-late 4 us." This was a huge bonus for me to do my first full fledged translation for a POW.

---

[39] Watch our back

After considerable snoop'n and poop'n, we were all able to crouch down and move forward for a little bit. Finally, the other marine stood up and stuck out his hand to me. "Great job out there, Corporal. The bad guy was spooked a bit at first and maybe wondering if it was some sort of a trap. But when you guys started whispering back and forth, he couldn't resist trying to make the shot. I think that he figured that you guys were just off the airplane and an easy shot at that time. It was damn risky on your part, because he might have not been alone, but it all worked out just great for our side. He was actually set up just a rock-throw from us, so we decided to capture him instead of slitting his throat. This way, there was no gunshot, and his friends won't have a clue that he will be spilling his guts to us. The intel people will love us for making the capture, and, even though he isn't a NVA professional, he will be fun for the spooks to play with for a while."

When we moved to where the prisoner was being held, we were introduced to the rest of the counter-sniper team, and there sat the victim of stupidity and greed.

He was a young man, maybe twenty years old. He had been armed with a Soviet-made SKS rifle that was sporting a halfway-decent, Chinese-made scope.

The enemy soldier was sitting with his hands tied behind him around a tree. This position would dislocate one or both shoulders with just the slightest movement. Even so, his pain was silenced by the duct tape that was tightly wrapped around his head, covering his eyes. I asked to have it cut away from his eyes so I could watch them as I spoke with him. Even the Vietnamese tended to look down when they lie.

Fear, terror, and pain were all quite evident in his eyes as they darted back and forth to each one of us as. Apparently, he was attempting to decide who could become his savior or perhaps his executioner.

I cleared my voice to try and sound more official to the POW. *"Ban co Viet Congf hay quan troung xuyen?"*[40] My question went unanswered, because his mouth was still sealed with the duct tape. Now the fear doubled in his eyes as he realized that, not only could I speak to him, but he could not play that I-don't-understand-you card.

"Neu ban khong noi voi nhung Marines se lani cho cai chet cva ban mat Nhieu ngay. Toi chi co the giup ban ngay bay gio. Lan ban hieu toi?"[41]

The man nodded his head yes as he began to tremble and tears now came rolling from his eyes to his cheeks.

I tore the tape from his mouth, peeling the skin off his lips as I did so. There was no gentle way of removing it after it had been put on and pressed down several times. Lumps of coagulated blood immediately began to form on his lips, pouring down his chin, soaking his shirt and pants. Flies appeared out of nowhere and soon covered the crusting blood in a swarm of buzzing filth.

I remembered Jack Webb in the movie *The DI*. He would stand feet apart and hands on his hips when he spoke. That left an impression on me, and so I thought, what the hell, I do the same thing.

"Neu ban chuyen chan Tralac ho toi ban se nhin thay ngay mai. Neu ban chon se duoc stupid. Ban se tim thay ban da chet nhu the nay vao ngay mai. Ban lua chon!"[42]

I suppose he felt the same fear I would have felt if it had been me that had just been captured by them—except he did have a choice,

---

[40] "Are you Viet Cong or regular army?"
[41] "If you don't speak with me now, these Marines will make your death last for many days. *Do you understand me?*"
[42] "If you talk honestly and answer me now, you may see tomorrow. If you choose to be stupid, your friends will find you dead, tied like this tomorrow. This is your choice!"

and I would have died a slow and painful death regardless. It was difficult for me to find very much compassion for the man who had just been my hunter. He was there, watching and waiting to send me home in a casket if I would have lost this contest. Compassion has no place for the enemy in war, neither giving nor receiving—or so I was finding out.

"*Nai nao bay den tu? Ban co tu phia bac hoac nam Viet Nam?*"[43] Once his bravado had broken and disappeared, he took on the look of a child fearing the worst possible punishment from us. He was scared for his life now, and that was a good thing.

"*Toi tumiern Nam Sai Gon. Toi six Te En tuai chi.*" As he spoke to me, I translated to the counter-sniper team. He said "He is from the south; near Saigon. He is just eighteen years old."

I paused, staring into his fear-filled eyes, "*Ban da co mot vo va gin dinh. Va ban muon xem lai? Neu ban muon xem lai co mot nguoi dan ong va khong phai la mot anh hung lam tinh.*"[44]

His eyes were intently dark and void of any contempt as they carefully followed mine. I stood and walked around him as I spoke. "*Do la do no va no se la dieu do se buid ban con hoang dia hoi Viet. Chung toi khong phai la ting phap. Hong choi tro chai voi chung toi hoac ban se duoc chet trong mot giay lat.*"[45] As I said that to him, I kicked his taped ankles hard to help reinforce my point and to maintain my Jack Webb image.

I think that I had convinced him that talking and living would be a better choice than to become a dead hero. This boy warrior had already cried and pissed himself, but I made no mistake that he

---

43 "Where do you come from? Are you from North or South Vietnam?"
44 "Do you have a wife and family you wish to see again? If you do want to see them again, try to be a man and not a fucking hero."
45 "It is that it is and it shall be that it shall be, you Viet Cong bastard. We are not the French, so don't play games with us or you will be dead in just one more moment."

would have killed me, and there were always plenty more like him where he'd come from.

Dead is dead, and the age or maturity of the sender was of no consequence when you are in your grave. He was scared only because he had been caught, and not because he was a killer of marines.

Snatch and I left him to be taken along as a POW by the two sergeants of the counter- sniper team. I never bothered to follow up and see if he in fact made it to the rear or not. Sometimes unfortunate accidents will happen, and there are escape attempts in which the person dies, but then again, this man could potentially be a wealth of information. At any rate, the situation was beyond what I had just done, so my job was over and done with.

Snatch whimpered and whined all of the way back to our admin office, where he promptly requested future duty digging pissers and shitters rather than going on another recon mission. *Con hoang khong co quay tron!*[46]

---

46 *Spineless bastard!*

Chapter 6

When I got back to our tent, the salts had already tagged me with "Zapper," or *Su Sin Dong*, and Doc Fox now became "Dead Eye Doc," or *Chet Mat Bac Si*. We had a "Wetting-down party" for our first kill in the field, which started in our tent and then continued at the NCO club. Sergeant Morley sauntered over to our table to ask if he could cop a squat[47] for a bit. Because he didn't smoke or drink, we knew that, after a couple of Cokes, he'd boogie back to his hooch to write his wife and family a letter.

Most of us had just graduated from high school or college, but the difference here was about killing or being killed, not where we'd go cruising tonight or double date. I thought that, when I had some time in grade,[48] Staff Sergeant O'Donnell and Sergeant Morley were just what I wanted to be like when I grew up. These two guys were the real deal.

A couple of times, I let Doc Fox take the trigger, and I'd spot for him, but John just never had the killer instinct he needed to be a true sniper. There were a couple of shots I knew he could have taken,

---

[47] Sit
[48] Time accumulated in that rank

but he would always stand down just before popping the cap. I guess that must have come along with his MOS of a corpsman, because he was always out there, helping others—and believe me, he was damned good at that too.

Doc Fox had pulled out all of the stops more than once to save a marine from going home in the silver box. There was no doubt in my military mind that he'd take a bullet or jump on a live grenade to save another person's life. A corpsman may be navy officially, but if you ask any marine about a corpsman, he or she will loud sing praise for him. Doc, and that is any *Bac si*, will always be revered by the grunts.

Our own Doc Fox had become quite the storyteller too. Of course, they were not always personal events involving him, but fiction sometimes based on fact. They were always entertaining, and each story carried a stone-hard message of some sort. The boots especially enjoyed listening, and learning from him.

One story I loved hearing him tell was about the time he was out on a patrol with Lima Company of the Third Battalion, Third Marine Regiment. They were conducting a search-and-destroy sweep through a known North Vietnamese held area.

Doc had been following the marine in front of him through the eight-foot-tall elephant grass, while keeping a safe and normal interval between each man. If you got too close and screwed up your interval, a tripped booby trap might mean more than just him getting wounded or zapped. The only problem with interval in elephant grass was the possibility of losing sight of the marine to your front or rear.

John became momentarily distracted by the marine behind him, who was asking for some APCs.[49] As he turned back toward his front, he saw his lead man now double-timing off to the left

---

[49] Aspirins

from the path that they had just been on. At this point, Doc was just able follow the moving grass and the sound as best he could. Unfortunately, he was never actually able to see the man who was now running full out ahead of him.

They were still on a thinly veiled path, but it appeared to be getting larger and more used the more they continued on it. Just as it began to break into an open area, Doc finally got his first good look at the man he had been following—he was wearing a khaki uniform with the distinctive pith helmet of a North Vietnamese soldier, complete with an AK-47 in his hands.

Apparently, when John turned back to hand APCs to the man behind him, the enemy soldier ran right to left, crossing the path that the marines were on. After having seen his potential blunder, the enemy soldier broke into a full sprint, hoping that he had not been spotted by any of the marines.

John said he quickly applied his brakes and made a screeching U-turn as the soldier he had been following began shouting to other enemy soldiers. Doc wasn't sure if the enemy was telling them about his close call with the American that was following him or what, but he sure wasn't going to hang around to find out. Fox went on to describe his record-breaking, mad dash back toward where the marine lines in great, animated detail.

When Petty Officer Fox finally made contact with friendlies again, he was with a completely different marine unit. After relating his encounter to the men in the new platoon, he was summarily presented with the unofficial, but marine-grunt certified DFM[50] complete with dingleberry clusters.

John would retain the homemade DFM with clusters as one of his fondest possessions from his tour in 'Nam. The medal itself was cut from a flattened aluminum beer can and then painted. "DFM"

---

50 Dumb-fuck medal

was then scratched onto it, and some sort of colorful material was draped from the supporting ribbon. It was generally hung around the wearer's neck, like the Medal of Honor would be.

This wasn't really such a funny story unless you watched and heard it being told by this six-foot-three, two-hundred–and-twenty-pound wannabe comedian. Each time I heard him tell it, the medal became bigger and better, and his DFM with clusters grew fancier than it actually ever was.

Chapter 7

I sat down and ate morning chow with a helicopter crew chief, Staff Sergeant Peter Connor,[2] and I listened to his salty tales about his being a door gunner in the Huey. That was all pretty exciting stuff to me, so when he asked me if I wanted to go along on a flight with them at 1100 today, I didn't have to think about an answer. "Hell yeah, I want to go along!"

The Huey was scheduled to take mail and a couple of needed parts out to an LPH 8, *Valley Forge*, a ship that was sitting about fifteen miles off of the coast. These missions where there was little or no chance of enemy encounter were known to the aviation marines and grunts as milk runs.

"This is generally a piece-of-cake flight for us, and more'n half the time we don't even take an assistant gunner along. But then too that sorta depends on who is flying, because there are a couple of pilots that are still bucking for their air-medal count. When they fly, we'll go out the long way to see if we can pick up some enemy ground fire so we can call that particular milk run as an actual combat flight. If that be the case, you can take the port gun, but I wouldn't sweat it."

It sounded like something really different, and it would be fun just to get up and off the ground for a while. "Can we take another passenger with us? Our corpsman was supposed to go out to the range and requalify on the M-60 machine gun today, so this will give him the ticket he needs to have for that particular weapon system."

"Not a problem, Corporal. We have plenty of room, so bring him along. We generally eat noon chow on the Happy Valley while they top off our fuel tanks, and then we just head on back. If we cruise around again looking for a scrap, it could be a bit longer before landing, so don't set yerself an ETA[51] back here. Be at pad thirteen about ten thirty, and we'll do the preflight check together."

I double-timed all the way back to the hooch, excited with the prospect of a laid-back afternoon just enjoying an uneventful flight and some navy chow on the LPH. I already knew about the *Valley Forge* or "Happy Valley," because my dad flew off her during WWII when she was still a CVA, or light aircraft carrier. She was still a big ship, but was dwarfed by current aircraft carriers of today and was converted to a helicopter-only ship that could deploy marines ashore for an emergency call for help somewhere, be it the Atlantic or Pacific Ocean.

Now I was most definitely looking forward to this flight as a change of pace from my green oven of a tent, the dirt, dust, bugs, and, of course, the open-air shitters and stinking piss tubes.

*   *   *

John was busy cleaning the M-14 when I barged into the tent. "Hey Doc, do you want to do something really cool and different this afternoon? I got us an invite to fly out to the Valley Forge for a milk run. We have to be at helipad thirteen at 10:30, if you want to go along. I'm going to go for sure, so I just have to hustle on over to

---

[51] (Estimated time of arrival

admin and let them know what the scoop is. You should be able to get your A-ticket qualification for the M-60 while we are out over the water too."

Doc was pumped up at the prospect of the flight, and he started getting his brain bucket and flak jacket to take along for the ride in the Huey.

I laughed and said, "I don't think there is a real need for those things, Doc, because this is going to be just another routine milk run. Besides, we will be flying over water, so we will have to wear a Mae West and I don't think I'd like to wear one over my flak jacket or a helmet. If you sink, yer screwed, blued, and tattooed!"

John laughed too. "I heard that the grunts sit on their flak jackets so they don't catch a stray round coming up through the floor. Then they could get wounded in a certain part that they'd rather not be shot in. I can just see me years after the war talking with my kid: 'Daddy, daddy … where did you get wounded when you were in the war?'"

His voice deepened as he got his sober expression on his face. "'Well, son, I was shot in the ass, and then I had my pecker shot off.'"

I was laughing my ass off at this big, dumb-shit corpsman as he became very animated when he was into this comedic character of his. When I finally caught my breath, I said "So if you got your pecker shot off in the war, Daddy, who the hell is the father of your son?"

He never missed a beat when he said, "That damn mailman was delivering both the male and the mail to my wife. She forgot who I was because I was away at war. Men all look alike down there to women, or so I'm told."

*   *   *

Staff Sergeant Connor was peering into the open engine cowling of the Huey when we got to pad thirteen. "If the baling wire holds this bucket together, we may actually be able to make a round trip again. The Marine Corps buys these old crashed birds that have been recycled from the army scrap heap, you know?"

John and I both looked at each other at the same time, wondering—or at least hoping—he was just bullshitting us. These wing wipers[52] had sort of a different kind of humor.

"Okay, you two ground-pounders, let's go over a couple of things before we take to the sky like Superman does." There were just a few things he had to cover, because we would be flying over water, and we were actually more like crew than marine ground-crunchers being taken out someplace to be dumped off on a one-way ride to an LZ.[53]

I was going to man the portside gun while we were over land, and then Fox could take over and run a belt or two through over the water, and then he'd get his qualification ticket up to snuff.

The pilot and copilot showed up to do their walk around flight check with Staff Sergeant Connor and to make sure that the two dozen mailbags aboard had been secured properly. They were cool about us going along for the ride, but they said we were going to take the "High Road" on the way out and back in.

Connor just looked at us, smiled a lame grin, and shook his head back and forth.

"Aw, shit, another one of those gungy snoop-and-poop, oh-please-shoot-at-me-flights," he mumbled. "At least you guys will get to see some countryside, and, as I recall, we don't get paid by the hour."

Of course, I put on a flight helmet so I could hear and talk to the two drivers[54] and the crew chief. We snagged an extra brain bucket so Doc could plug in and join us, rather than listening to the *thump*,

---

52 Aviation marines
53 Landing Zone
54 Pilots

thump, thump of the twin rotor blades chewing up the air. This was just so different, so fun and exciting to take us away from the hum-drum, same-ol'-shit routine of twenty-four/seven.

This was only my second ride in the Huey, because the marines still had a shit pot full of the older Sikorsky UH-34 Choctaws. I think that the first angels were issued those old 34s back during Korea. They were good birds for their time, but their time was now long past.

We were about twenty minutes out of Da Nang when the copilot said, "Okay, you two on the guns back there, let's look alive, cause we've got beaucoup green tracers coming up at us at our two o'clock low. Lets lock and load while we go in to have a look-see so we can advise the gunships of the possible target."

The bad guys had the green tracers, and we had the red tracers, so it would look like Christmas with the greens coming up and the reds going down.

"Oooohrah, some air action!" I said to no one.

The situation changed instantly, and the sky came blazingly alive with the green'ers coming up at us from all over the frigg'n place. They looked like lights or balls as they originated from what seemed to be a thousand different places. Each tracer that was visible only accounted for the other four that I couldn't see, so our pitiful dozen reds that were descending appeared to be almost comical in comparison.

"Oh, shit," Connor said over the intercom. "Look alive on the portside, grunt. We've got beaucoup enemy fire coming up at us; from all over the fucking place now, and some really big ones too!"

Yeah, Staff Sergeant, like I couldn't see the damn things myself. I had already wondered if maybe the VC or NVA had just fired a few sucker rounds at us to get us to come over and investigate. When the sneaky little bastards lured you in close enough, they drop that big "oh shit" hammer on you. This was a trick they used on the ground all the time, and we quickly became aware and cautious of that trap. So, was this supposed to be something new that the zoomies hadn't seen before? Obviously these two officers had never read the book about the French and the Viet Minh in the Ashau Valley in 1953. Fuck … me … hard—we'd just been lured in for one big sucker punch.

Connor sounded almost mesmerized, as he was now hanging out of the door and looking around. "Uh-oh, skipper, there are some even bigger guns shooting at us and they look like maybe they are 37s. Where in the fuck did 37s come from because there ain't supposed to be any of them anywhere in country?" Thirty-seven-millimeter anti-aircraft guns were true aircraft killers—not that their 12.7s were BB guns to be unconcerned about, but these were the bad that belonged in bad news. They wouldn't just shoot down a slow-moving helicopter; they'd blow the sucker clear out of the sky!

The three crew members were now jaw-jacking all at the same time, and I just kept on smoking the barrel of my machine gun. The entire jungle below us now had become one big-ass target.

I was swinging the machine gun wildly in its mount as I tried to answer back to each point where I could see tracers or muzzle flashes originating. This was definitely pumping my adrenalin through my veins at max speed, and, while it was beaucoup exciting, it was a li'l bit intimidating all at the same time.

I supposed this was right up there along with stepping over the side of the thirty-five-foot rappelling tower for the first time. It scared the crap out of me until I was actually over the side, and then it became fun—scary, but it was fun once it was done and behind you.

The thing was, this Huey bird could fall out of the sky like it was a BFR[55] if the wrong part of the aircraft took a critical hit. There was close to an adrenalin overdose pumping, as well as our 7.62s, as

---

[55] Big fucking rock

our Huey nosed up hard and laid over on its side so we could *chay nhu dia ngiec*.[56]

The pilot was trying to put some quick altitude between us and the ground, when I both heard and felt the 12.7-millimeter enemy rounds hitting the bottom of our bird in rapid succession.

Thud, thud …. thud …. thud! The big bullets were ripping through the lower deck and then whizzing right back out the top like there was nothing there to even try and slow them down. At least none of the five of us got in the way of one of the bullets as they came and went whizzing through the thin aluminum skin of the aircraft.

"All right, you guys back there, we took some hits, but we have moved out of their range for now and we're breaking for the safety of the open water."

I wondered if I really needed a lieutenant to tell me that four big-ass bullets just came smoking up the crack of my ass and back out the top of the bird. Not that it was any kind of a big deal; it just seemed sort of ironic and stupid at that particular moment.

The open water was a good thing too, because both of our ammo cans were now as dry as popcorn farts. About the only thing left for us to do beyond this point was to piss out the door on the zipper-heads down there.

The pilot continued after a brief pause, "Well, okay … some bad news now too. It appears as if we are losing hydraulic pressure and fuel at a pretty quick rate."

"What the fuck?" I mumbled to myself. I thought someone told me that these Huey Birds had self-sealing fuel tanks and redundant hydraulics. Ah, the low bidder for our weapons of war once again. That was probably an option that was only available on the newer-version Huey, not the one I was in.

---

56 Run like hell.

The voice in my earphones very calmly stated, "We are going to try and make the LPH, but we may go feet wet before we can achieve our goal. Be ready! It will be close … I think, maybe. If we can." John and I both threw wide-eyed looks at each other. "Feet wet," he mouthed.

Now there was a tad bit more urgency in the voice as it said; "Okay back there, we are going down on the surface of the water. Just in case we have put her down, prepare for ditching."

Wait a minute, I thought. The staff sergeant didn't cover this ocean-landing-and-ditching shit in our briefing. I turned to Doc, who was looking back at me with apparently the same question that was double-timing through my gourd. I turned back toward the crew chief as he was pulling his machine gun out of the mount and pitching it out of the door and into the ocean below us.

That's when it really hit home that this was really for real and not some training bullshit. My headset rang out with the pilot on the radio saying, "Mayday … Mayday … Mayday!"

"Oh shit … Oh shit … Oh shit," was simultaneously streaking through my brain-housing group! I might have thought it out loud or I might have thought it to myself, but I distinctively remember, "I'm not having much fun right now, and this so-called milk-run flight is starting to suck a big time *hachi*!"

The pilot's voice was calm once again, as if this was something he'd practiced saying a dozen times. "It's going to be really, really close, you guys back there. Pitch everything we don't need off of the bird, and then prepare for a water-ditching. We may become a rock very soon!"

I looked back over to the crew chief once again. Why didn't that asshole cover ditching and crashing or any of that other scoop with us? "Milk run" my aching, grunt ass!

I wondered if I'd have to pay the Marine Corps back for the M-60 as I pitched it out the door. I watched the 23 pound gun fall until it crashed into the blue ocean water, barely missing an LBGB.[57] *Oi ohoi oi*. I smiled as I thought, that'll screw up our community relations for today. *Xin Loi*, y'all!

A voice came from up front again. "We now have a visual on the ship, so cross your fingers."

Screw that, I thought, because I'm not the one that is flying this shot up chopper. You two guys up front cross your frigg'n fingers, because we have to follow along where ever it is that you two take us.

I turned again to John, and he had a look of one pretty unhappy sailor that was just about to go for a swim in the ocean. His lips were moving, but he wasn't saying anything that I could hear, so I hoped that he was praying for us to make that ship.

"Okay now, we're getting close and I'm going up to try and make that flight deck. Wait! … Waittt! … Okay … Okayyy; Wait! … Wait! … We're on deck! Vamos, get outta here, now!"

The flight deck of that ship looked like the golden streets of heaven to me as I leapt out of that chopper and onto something dry and solid. Just as my feet touched down, I could feel Fox slam into me from behind, and he knocked me completely off of my feet. That was actually a good thing he just had done for me, because he was then hit full on by a stream of foam coming from fire hoses.

I watched him as he went rolling along in front of me, just before both of us were snatched up and pulled away by the crash crew in big silver fire suits who had come wading into our midst.

These navy zoomies had their shit together, and they worked like they were a team of one person with many hands. It would have been cool to watch all of this, but not so cool to be the ones that were being watched.

Once we were out of harm's way, I felt like I was going to pee

---

[57] Little bitty gook boat

myself—not that I needed to, I guess, but just because I could. Maybe that was an instinctive reaction to stress?

I scrambled over next to the copilot and I excitedly said, "Wow, that was pretty close back there, sir. I guess you guys must have cut the engines off just in the nick of time, huh?"

He looked at me very matter-of-factly and said, "Marine, we didn't cut off the engine. She quit on her own because we were out of fuel!"

It took a moment for that to soak into my grunt mentality, but then I got what he was telling me. That sucker quit on us because we ran out of fuel! Wow, no shit, Sherlock! It can't get any closer than that!

When we finally got down to the chow hall, neither John nor myself were hungry anymore, even though the food aboard the ship appeared to be gourmet chow compared to what we usually ate.

Staff Sergeant Connor came over to our table and sat his overflowing tray down. "Wow, now that was pretty exciting stuff back there, huh? Man alive, I've never seen so much ground fire coming up at us as we had today; and if those were, in fact, 37s, that'll be a first too. Gee, maybe we just became an important part of history."

I looked up at him to see if he was kidding me or what. "Part of history because we got shot at by something bigger and different?" I said back to his joyful, yet serious, expression. Maybe I was the only one that was able to see the irony in his words, but I smiled back at him and nodded my head in agreement anyway.

"I don't know if you or I hit anything down there today groundpounder, but I hear that Spooky sent Puff the Magic Dragon over to breathe some hellfire down on them. But I also heard that even those guys were turned back, because of the heavy ground fire. I'll bet now they'll divert an arc-light strike tonight. Them ol' B-52s will put a serious hurt locker full of bombs in the sky that'll even snuff out the bugs crawling around."

Now we would have to spend the night aboard the Happy Valley, because we had no choice but to wait for a scheduled ride back to Da Nang and our unit tomorrow. This was a going to be a serio[58] treat for John and myself to actually be able to go ten toes in a real rack (bed) with a real mattress, clean sheets, and even an authentic pillow. How sweet it is!

That night they had a flick in the hanger bay, and some marine that was on mess duty made up some unauthorized fudge that was actually fresh, unlike the brown rocks we'd get in our month-old care package from home. I was ready to transfer over for this kind of life aboard ship, and I didn't feel one bit sorry or guilty about spending a night here in Camelot—not one bit sorry!

The next morning, at zero nine hundred, we were supposed to hitch our ride back to Da Nang, but the chopper didn't actually leave the LPH until closer to noon. *Dien hinh len va cho doi nhanh.*[59]

We were all going to be shuttled back on a cargo chopper, and hopefully they would not be going out and looking for hostile action on the way. One ride on the high road was sufficient for at least this week.

---

58 Serious
59 Typical. Hurry up and wait.

Chapter 8

When we got back to our tent area at about 1300, things appeared to be suspiciously calm for that time of the day.

"Something big is going on, Zapper; it's way too quiet," Doc quickly said.

I was just about to say the same thing, but, as we turned the corner, we immediately knew what the answer was to the still atmosphere.

There at the hatchway of our tent were two rifles stuck into the ground by their bayonets and a camo-covered helmet sitting on the butt of each rifle. Two pairs of jungle boots were facing backward. That was supposed to be symbolic of death, someone said at one time. I remembered that being done on JFK's riderless horse at his funeral. I recall this, because I wrote an essay in high school about the subject. For some reason, the story of that caparisoned horse[60] stuck with me more than anything else.

Doc and I both looked at each other, not even believing what we were actually seeing. Both of our tent mates, Private First Class Dan Jackson and Lance Corporal Brian Rodriquez, had not returned to

---

[60] A single riderless horse that follows the caisson with boots reversed in the stirrups

their pick-up point at the designated time and place. Consequently, they had been listed as MIA, effective as of 0800 today.

The two of them had been out observing enemy movements on the Ho Chi Minh trail for the last two days and nights. This area was rich in intelligence, because of the large amount of enemy vehicle and foot traffic that was observed heading south on the road.

The information that was gathered there provided information that was difficult to obtain using camera optics from RF-4 Phantom jets. They were fitted with side-looking airborne radar and IR[61] sensors. None of these three was capable of penetrating the triple-canopy jungle—although there were some marginal readouts from the IR, that is, if the target was hot enough to "bloom" on film.

When all the high-tech things couldn't or wouldn't work, the eyes and ears fell back on those who were trained to gather it the old-fashioned way, and that was the recon marine. Their job was long, tedious, exhausting, and extremely dangerous. They had to be very close to the road to covertly observe and report the numbers of the enemy's coming and goings. Sometimes they were close enough to actually hear them talking to one another, and that could also be a bonus.

Although these marines were well camouflaged, they remained in harm's way from the very beginning to the absolute end of each mission. They used the stealth of a sniper to come and go during the cover of night. Often, they would be crawling on their bellies for hour after hour and for mile after mile.

As a lance corporal with less than two years in the Marine Corps, I was paid $121.30 a month, plus $65.00 for combat pay. $186.30 wasn't very much to be getting paid for being shot at, but we certainly had no control over that. We were marines doing what marines did best, and marines get shot at sometimes. Amen!

After the two of them had gone MIA, other recon marines

---

[61] Infrared

volunteered to out looking for them. It isn't like you can just go trudging about the boonies calling their names, because they had gone very deep into Indian Country.[62]

Staff Sergeant Larry O'Donnell and Sergeant Joe Morley were the ones who went on the rescue mission, and about two hours into it, they stumbled upon a full-company-sized patrol of NVA. That meant that they were probably outnumbered more than twenty to one. Both of these outstanding marines were killed in action while taking at least twenty or more of the enemy, who were seen lying dead near them. They were spotted by an army O-1-E Bird-dog airplane that had joined in the rescue attempt.

Apparently, as they were being overrun by the enemy, they had called Broken Arrow on the radio for all artillery and close air support to be dropped right in on their own position. Their radio went dead when the napalm covered them.

Later in the day, our grunts recovered four Chieu Hoi deserters from the enemy forces. These four South Vietnamese civilians had been conscripted to carry supplies from Hanoi to someplace in South Vietnam. They were able to slip away and were trying to go back home when they were captured.

Two of the four said they had seen two American prisoners brought down off of a hill earlier yesterday morning. The Chieu Hois said both men had been severely beaten before they were each summarily tied to the back of a truck and dragged away while they were still alive. The captured men agreed that there could be little or none of their bodies left to recover. Besides, the final destination of the trucks was unknown.

With that information and the location that they provided, there could be no doubt of the identities of those two marines as the missing Jackson and Rodriquez.

---

62 Enemy held area

Staff Sergeant O'Donnell had been on his second tour in country, and Sergeant Morley was on his first. Both of these men had their previous tours in grunt outfits before voluntarily becoming recon marines. Our two tent mates, Jackson and Rodriquez, were both on their first tour, with less than a month in country, before being killed.

Doc and I never really got to know much about them because they had been here for such a short time and it seemed that either the two of us were out in the bush or they were.

I know that Brian had been married for just a short time before being deployed to Vietnam, and that he'd just found out the other day that his eighteen-year-old wife was pregnant. He would get a perfumed, SWAK letter every single day without fail from her.

Dan Jackson was single, but he had a brother who was a Green Beret, someplace in the III Corps area. Of course, his brother wouldn't be escorting his younger brother's body home for burial, because there was no body to escort.

With the deaths of O'Donnell and Morley, it really hit home to each of us that we were all subject to being killed at any time, regardless of our expertise. These two marines were the people who were teaching us not to make mistakes out there; and they got zapped! I guess that sometimes you just step into something big, deep, and unexpected, and the shit is too deep for you to keep your head up and above it.

What more could ever demonstrate what marines are made of then when calling Broken Arrow directly on yourself. It was a suicide call for sure, and was mind-numbing for all of us to imagine.

Had John and I not ended up spending the night in the cush and comfort of the LPH, we would have both, most assuredly, volunteered and gone along on the rescue mission. I know, in my own military mind, that I would have teamed up with my two mentors just to live and learn from the best.

Talk about fate!

Yeah, give them a medal and a silver box home. *Ten cua ban thang nam sinh vinh hang hoi nhung auh hung toi.*[63]

When we went back into our tent, the belongings of Dan Jackson and Brian Rodriquez were already sanitized, and their stuff was packed for shipment back home.

All hands attended the service for the four of them in the chapel that evening, but only Staff Sergeant O'Donnell and Sergeant Morley were already confirmed as KIA. Both Jackson and Rodriquez would be carried on the rolls as MIA for the time being. Now there were four inverted rifles with helmets set on the butt and boots pointing backward. I wondered if the enemy soldiers did this same type of thing when they lost their friends or family.

When the service was finished, most of us sat in the chow hall for a while and theorized about what had gone wrong and how they had been captured or killed. Of course, there would never be an answer to any of these questions, because those who did know for sure were all dead. We were then off to the club, where we all got thoroughly and completely wasted to celebrate our life—or the possibility of our own impending death. Alcohol blurs everything, so we didn't have to deal with it until sometime later in our life. Maybe back stateside it would all finally go away once and for all.

I passed out someplace between two tents close to the club. I finished my night Z'd out and puking on myself. The fire watch finally found me and literally drug my stinking, sorry ass back to my hooch.

Fox and I continued to go out on missions together whenever we could, but more frequently, he was being called upon to go out on larger operations while I was working alone whenever possible.

Trust during combat is something that is difficult just to hand

---

[63] May your names last forever some place, my heroes.

over to another person. It isn't about liking or knowing them—it is about sharing thoughts and unspoken communications.

My parents spoke of married people sharing thoughts like this after having been together for years. For us, it was a bond—like being a twin, I suppose. If I could explain this kind of Zen, or if I was able to teach it in a classroom, I'd be writing a bestselling book and counting the big bucks that I'd made from it.

Chapter 9

Our tour was now starting to wind down, and we were counting the days toward our twelfth month in country. It was very easy at that point to become FIGMO,[64] but too many guys let their guard down, and they got hurt. We had both skated on getting wounded thus far, so "heads up" was still the word of the day!

I'd traded off a NVA pith helmet to an admin pogue to arrange John's and my rotation date to fall on the same day. It would be so cool for us to catch the freedom bird back to Travis Air Force Base together.

The very next morning, our company gunny came swooping into our hooch to tell me that I was going to be attached to the Fifth Marines for a while. He actually kept a straight face when he told me that too. *A while* was normally a very loose and general term, meaning "until they were damn good and ready to release you back to your unit."

Here I'm now a short-timer that is so damn short that I can sit on a dime and dangle my feet! In fact, I was so frigg'n short I had to look up just to see the whale shit that was at the bottom of the ocean!

---

[64] Fuck it, got my orders!

"Hey, Gunny," I mused, "I thought I was supposed to be cut a huss[65] when I got short. What's the scoop on that, because I'm officially a short timer as we speak?"

He didn't even crack a smile when he said, "Oh, for Christ's sake, Corporal McMullin, you sound like you are an air force whiner. This is just a frigg'n milk run, so just go with the flow, marine. You'll probably be back here in a few days, so hold your alligator tears or go and see the chaplain. He might actually give a shit and drop a dime for you."

Khong co di ia.[66] Did he have to say it was another milk run? The last time I heard that terminology applied, the milk got pretty damn sour before that particular mission had played out.

Doc was to stay in the rear with the gear, while I was off to some operation with exaggerated body counts. If I actually had the number that was generally reported for me, I'd have been the top sniper in all of the Republic of Vietnam. No one could possibly ever believe that, while I was out there by myself, I would accumulate six or more KIA in one day. Those numbers were far and few between as a sniper.

Most of the time, I'd likely be sitting on top of some sandbagged bunker within a crummy firebase. I seldom saw a nice, clean target, but I would try to shoot at a puff of smoke or a muzzle flash just out of pure-ass boredom. Who knows if I ever got the bastard, because the enemy was famous for dragging off the dead and wounded so any real body count was just blowing smoke up someone's ass.

Late that afternoon, I left with a supply convoy of ten six-bys.[67] I was going to position myself some distance from a two man artillery

---

65 Given favor
66 No shit
67 Six-by-six cargo trucks

FO[68] team. They were part of a battery of 105s[69] and 155s[70] that were hopefully going to catch a couple of enemy trucks out on the open road so we could blow them up. I was along to clean up the loose ends that may have survived the big bang.

The FOs, of course, had each other, and a radio, while all I had my ghillie suit, rifle, .45 pistol, and a KA-Bar knife.

When we finally reached a spot that we all liked, we all clambered off of the truck. I made my own way up into the trees, while the FOs headed up to wherever it was that they wanted to be. I'd made my own ghillie suit, and, with it on, I was damn near impossible to be seen when I was hunkered down.

Americans weren't the only ones that drove this road, but each side usually attempted to not run into each other at the same time. That wasn't normally a problem, either, because we traveled mostly by daylight, and they liked to use the cover of darkness.

As darkness settled in, I could hear some movement down on the road below me, but I couldn't get a clear shot because the clouds were covering the moon. Without the moonlight, I didn't stand a chance in hell of acquiring a positive target, so I just hunkered down. I had to wait for another clean-shot opportunity to come along providing, the cloud cover dissipated.

I was pretty much screwed to obtain a target, and I was wishing that I had one of the newfangled, talked-about, night-viewing devices. As we said, "You can wish in one hand and shit in the other," because the army got all of the new stuff way before marines even dreamt of seeing it.

It was just about 0515 when a small convoy of three Russian-made Gaz-51 trucks came cruising down the road. They stopped at a small bridge to look at a map, and I was able to bring my scope on

---

68 Forward observer
69 Big guns
70 Bigger guns

an NVA officer as he walked over to take a piss off of the bridge. I figured that he must be the HFMIC,[71] because he was waving his arms around and pointing here and there as he shouted orders to the snuffies. *Thanks for the confirmation*, I thought as I took up the slack on the trigger. While he was standing there with his dick in his hand and a cigarette between his lips, I put a round right between his shoulder blades. That set him rocking forward enough to cause him to do a double-gainer into the stream below. Not very many men can say that they died with their dick in their hand and a cigarette in their mouth. Semper Fi!

Because of the hills that were surrounding us, the sound of my shot echoed enough that no one knew exactly which side of the hill I was on, let alone my precise position. It was complete pandemonium as the NVA troops began to run all over the place, pointing at and shooting at just whatever they thought looked like an enemy sniper.

I was just placing my crosshairs on another officer who was shouting and pointing when the sky came alive with the shrieking of one of our own artillery rounds that was being called in by the forward observers.

This first one was coming way, way, *way* too frick'n close to my own position—probably because some numb-nutted, cannon-cocking, pecker-head draftee had not paid any attention to the correct powder charge and sent a long round off in my direction.

There is that fraction of a second when you hear that sucker coming at ya, like it was a big-ass freight train screeching through the sky, but there is not enough time to react. Incoming wasn't something you needed to be trained to hear or understand. You already knew the immediate consequences that were going to follow.

The resulting explosion sent me flailing through the air like I was

---

71 Head motherfucker in charge

a limp-ass ragdoll. The smell of explosives and dirt that was kicked up around me filled the air, along with my eyes, nose, and mouth. Of course, the fact that I was able to be smelling or feeling anything at all would indicate that I was, possibly, probably, and hopefully still alive and kicking.

My Remington was probably trashed and nowhere to be seen anymore. I really didn't give a shit, because it was probably unserviceable now and of no use to anyone anymore. Shit! Accountability for it was the last thing on my mind right now, anyway. All I wanted to do was get the fuck out of Dodge City, in case Zorba the dumb shit sent another long round my way.

Maybe it wasn't really a mistake made by a cannon-cocker. The first round was to be observed by the forward observer and then corrected. This could have just been a really shitty day for me, but, for the moment, it didn't really matter.

It doesn't make any difference if it wass a 7.62 X 39 round or one of those big 155 artillery pieces with your name on it. It's always the one that says "To whom it may concern" that will be sending your broken-up ass back home.

The incoming artillery stopped pounding the NVA trucks as I made my way down the hill to the riverbed, which was upstream from where I had killed the officer.

I found a niche in the riverbank where I was able to hunker down to regain my bearings. I didn't know, at that point, exactly how I was going to get my sorry ass back to the designated pick-up point to hitch my ride back home.

As I attempted to move forward toward better cover and concealment, I realized that I had blood pouring down my left arm. I used my KA-Bar to cut the sleeve off of my ghillie suit, and then I could see that there was about a five-inch wound on my bicep that was about a half-inch deep.

Shrapnel is so sharp that it can make a clean cut through you like a scalpel, and, unless you die before your knees buckle, you still may not feel it. I was able to stop most of the bleeding with my first-aid packet, but I knew for sure that I now had to make that pickup point ASAP.

As I got closer to the road, I could hear the sound of some big trucks closing in on me. The deep rumble of the diesel engine told me they were our own six-bys and not those Soviet or Chinese-made Gaz or Zil trucks that were used by the NVA.

I came hauling ass out of the bushes right alongside the road to wave the lead truck down. That was when I saw the marine manning the machine gun swing it around and put me dead on in his sights. Just as he let loose a short burst in my direction, the truck driver slammed on the brakes, causing the rounds to hit the dirt in front of me and throwing the gunner clear of the gun mount.

Out-fucking-standing! Some gungy ass, dip shit, maggot-eating FNG thinks I look like a goddamned NVA soldier, so he is going to dust my ass off for me. *Ban con hoang ngu ngoc!*[72]

Okay, so maybe he couldn't tell who I was in my ghillie suit, but I sorta doubted that an enemy soldier that was dressed up like a big-ass bush would come running out in the middle of the road, trying to flag down a bunch of American trucks.

I guess I was not a happy camper at this moment. This was now my second break for the day, and I wasn't willing to push my luck any further.

My fortune turned for the better when I found that there were a couple of corpsmen aboard the trucks, so they patched me up, at least until I could get back into sickbay or the hospital to get stitches—then a hot shower and maybe some hot chow before getting in some serious rack time, with an assist of Mister Jack Daniels, of course.

Milk run, my now wounded and aching grunt ass! I guessed that,

---

[72] (You stupid bastard!)

on the positive side of this whole thing, I'd now be going home with a Purple Heart medal. I had to smile to myself when I recalled the joke about the marine that was going home with his "Purple Heart on!"

Tomorrow, maybe I could talk Doc into heading to the *ville* with me. He hated going to town, because, as soon as your warm butt hit the chair, the "tea ladies" were also copping a squat and telling you all about you're being their dream ticket back to the USA. "You numba one GI; you now buy me tea, GI? Lata then we go an make ah boom boom, then you like me fine then, GI. Okay now, you buy me ah tea now. Okay GI?"

If you didn't pay the exorbitant price for a shot glass of green tea, you suddenly became "You numba huck'n *ten*, GI! You ah numba huck'n *ten* cheap Charlie GI soma-bitch!"

Yeah, to me that all sounded like it was just one word coming out of them too. Ah, our love and lust came and went so fast in a skivvy house out there in the *ville*. Still, there was no way I was going to catch something from them now. I was way too short for that daily trip to the clap shack for my shot of penicillin. That shit would garner me an involuntary extension that was at, or for, the "convenience of the government."

Doc and I were now just three short days away from our shared rotation date. I was presented with my Purple Heart and a Navy Commendation Medal with the combat *V* device for valor. My brand new Sergeant stripes were also presented at the same formation. *How sweet it is!*

Doc was promoted to a much-deserved E-5, and he received the Navy Commendation Medal complete with a combat *V* and the Navy Achievement Medal.

These personal awards were in addition to all of the other fruit-salad ribbons that everyone got after they'd been in country for a year. There were only three ribbons that were worth a shit, though—

they were the CAR,[73] my Purple Heart, and the Commendation with the *V* for valor. Several medals can be presented with or without a combat *V* device. Civilians never know the difference but military people sure do, and that matters to me!

*　　*　　*

Our day had finally come at last, and we were sitting at the terminal in our moldy-smelling dress uniforms that had been stowed away for a year.

It was so convenient for them to send your already-packed-and-sanitized shit home when you were killed. All that was needed was for a friend to go through the things you had in your hooch. They took out the *Playboys* and all the other stroke books that were probably stashed in your footlocker. There were always the other personal things that Mom and Dad wouldn't really want to see.

---

[73] Combat action ribbon

Chapter 10

It felt very strange to be in our summer service uniforms rather than our usual tiger stripes. Now we spoke of our new adventures that were ahead for both of us. Forget the past year and look ahead to your future is what the people wanting us to reenlist said.

Dead Eye Doc was going to get out of the navy and go to college on his GI bill. Both of us chose to pass on our R and R trip out-of-country flight in order to save our money for stateside use. Too many guys went off to Bangkok, Hong Kong, Hawaii, or even Australia, just to come back dead-ass broke. Sure they had a ten-day drunk and got laid every night, but for the most part, they ran out of money long before they ran out of time.

I was able to purchase myself a new Chevy through the post exchange, and therefore beat the taxes I would have paid in the US. Of course, Doc wanted to save all of his money for school. It was strange that he didn't know what he wanted his major to be yet, but that would come once we were back in the real world of the round eyes.

I had orders to report to Marine Corps Base in Quantico, Virginia, after my thirty-day leave was up. My hometown held no new adventures for me, because all the girls from high school had gotten married, pregnant, or just gone away to college. The guys were either already in the service, away at college, or were off protesting the war to stay home and enjoy the privilege of peace and freedom. Besides, they were just kids, and I'd left that behind me someplace.

The year that we were gone seemed to have been frozen for us. But stateside, life continued to pass us by at light speed, so I felt like I was in a time warp.

I thought I'd pick up my new Chevy and then just cruise my way east, driving when and where I wanted to go, without being shot at.

Our chat of the future came to a sudden halt when we were all moved to the enclosed part of the terminal. "All right, you veterans. Everyone boarding Braniff flight 1369 will now remove all of your belongings and lay them out for a contraband inspection. If you have in your possession any explosives, ordinance, ammunition, firearms, drugs, narcotics, or any other kind of bullshit you shouldn't, you'll now have five minutes to dispose of it right over here. Those five minutes will be an amnesty period for you, and we will leave you during this time. If we come back and find any contraband or unauthorized items, you will be held accountable. That being the case, you will not make this or any future flight home. Every person of every rank will be checked, so don't be stupid in your last hour in country. Your time starts right now. Move it, people!"

Military men who should have known better began pulling stuff from sea bags, suitcases, and other baggage as they slithered over to the safe area to dispose of things they should have never had in their possession in the first place.

"Good Lord, Zap. Look at the shit people were going to carry on board with them," Dead Eye said.

"You gotta be shit'n me, Doc. That stupid fuckhead has an 81-mortar, HE heavy round. That POS thing could turn our airplane into a flying scrapheap falling out of the sky at thirty-three thousand feet." I wanted to jerk the guy up by his stacking swivel, unscrew the top of his gourd, and take a huge dump in it so he'd actually have something inside his stupid empty head!

It was incredible the number of prohibited items that accumulated there within five minutes. This stuff came from all ranks too, not just the enlisted guys, the majority, though, were E-4 and below. There were AK-47s, M-16s, even an M-14 rifle. Several handguns from both sides of the war and Lord knows what else was in the pile. What use could anyone possibly have with a fucking hand grenade at home? This kind of stuff was deadly, so why would you want to be taking it with you?

The pile of ammo that was accumulated there could have supported a daylong firefight out in the bush. "What in the hell is wrong with these stupid people, Zapper? They didn't get their fill of war toys during this last year?"

"Jeez, Doc," I said. "Most of these people never left the safe zone because they are a bunch of REMFs. Every damn one of them will go home telling the gory war stories of their bravest moments in combat. I'm sure they will be sporting a chestful of their PX medals too."

We all waited for the five minutes to pass so we could get the show on the frigg'n road.

"Hey, Zapper. I stowed away my medical kit, so do you think it is okay to still have with me?"

I laughed and said, "Hell yeah, John, you are *still* a corpsman aren't you? Just ditch the damn C-4[74] that you had in there for cooking C-Rations."

Each person was checked as promised and two numb-nutted army soldiers were led away by the military police for retaining some sort of contraband. "Probably was drugs of some sort," Doc said.

---

74 Plastic explosive

At last, we began boarding the baby-blue-colored Braniff freedom bird. At long last … we were really going back home to the land of the round eyes.

I sure was going to miss good ol' Specialist Cramer Haas and his "Goooooooood Morninggggggg, Vietnam" wakeup call on the radio each morning.

That wasn't necessarily so, Specialist Haas, but hey; thanks for being there and the smiles you gave all of us anyway!

As the airplane lifted off the runway, a cheer went up from every person on board. In an instant, the past twelve months slipped away behind us into what seemed to be a dream of epic proportions.

One day you are either the hunter, or the hunted—then you suddenly return to the life that was left behind you just a short while ago. Yesterday, I was wondering how much ammo and grenades to carry along with me on a patrol through Indian Country, and tomorrow, I will wonder what to eat next at the A&W—fries or onion rings?

The news about protesters, draft-card burning, and deserters fleeing to Canada were censored in the 'Nam. It wouldn't take long for the unpopularity of the war to become evident to us as we left the confines of Travis Air Force Base.

Protesters lined the street outside the main gate of the base, waiting for us to leave. Most were shouting baby-killer, warmonger, and other terms of endearment to us.

Americans were losing limbs or their lives just fourteen air hours away, just so that these scrotums would have the right to protest and spit on our bus. We are defending the right of these freaks to protest against us? Wow, how unique is America? Su dam me.[75]

At the San Francisco airport, Dead Eye Doc and the Zapper once again became Mister John Henry Fox and a very salty Sergeant Perry McMullin.

---

[75] Crazy

We were parting company and heading off into vastly different directions. John was going to college, where he'd probably never speak of saving or taking a human life again. I would remain a lifer after reenlisting in the Marine Corps. This would provide a certain return trip for me to Vietnam—probably one or more times someplace down the road.

Now came the time to say our parting words to each other. "Well, hey there, you jarhead; you Marine Corps lifer, I wish you a fair wind and following seas."

"Thanks, Doc, and Semper Fidelis; you are one of us, my trusted navy brother."

We parted with a handshake and a brief hug that we had each earned by our eternal membership into the silent and clandestine society of warriors.

Both of us vowed to remain in touch with each other, but in another brief moment, we would walk away in a different direction of life that was no longer shared between us. Our warrior bond was now irrevocably broken, and we shared only memories in a place where memories are seldom shared outside.

Chapter 11

"Good morning, Lieutenant. I'm Sergeant McMullin, Perry V. 1981844, reporting for duty according to my orders, sir."

"Good morning, Sergeant McMullin; we expected you here two days ago."

I ignored him because I could still count and I knew that I was actually reporting in two days early, not late.

Marine Corps Base Quantico was a picturesque place that existed primarily for the training of officers and some other areas of expertise for marines and law-enforcement people.

I was there to learn first and then to become an instructor teaching marines the skills of *Su ban va mot su giet.*[76]

Snipers had come into their own once again within the Marine Corps. Each different war found a need for trained and disciplined killers, but at the end of each war, snipers went into remission, and the skills faded from one generation of marines to another.

Peacetime did not necessitate the talents of the chosen few that actually saw their victim die from the pull of their trigger. Also, jobs for my qualifications were pretty far and few in the outside world.

---

[76] One shot and one kill

Once I had completed my training and the honing of my skills, which I had learned the hard way, I would at last become a coveted 0317 Marine Corps Sniper.

Marines like Carlos Hathcock, Eric England, and Chuck Mawhinney were the inspiration, icons, and *anh hung*[77] of the proud, the few, and the stealthy sniper. Military heroes are not long remembered by anyone but their brothers and sisters who reside within their ranks.

The war had now become so unpopular in the US that simply wearing a military uniform in public was cause to be berated, scorned, or just flat-ass spit on. The majority had become silent about the war, while the minority was now pretty much given free rein, press, and attention.

A few times, I thought about attempting to contact my former navy corpsman friend, but he probably had a beard on his face and hair that was growing down to his ass. I really doubted that he would sit and smoke grass with the war protesters, however, because he was proud of his military service. I'd retained the right to maintain that chip still firmly balanced on my shoulder, but that wasn't like John Fox to do that. He was the calm, deep thinker of the two of us, and that may be why we worked together as well as we did while we were in country.

The United States had changed a lot in a short time. College students had become a bunch of pukes living in the Emerald City, Land of Oz, without due regard to any discipline, reality, or sense of tomorrow. As the ocean quickly shrinks, America no longer enjoys her safety from attack, because our foreign enemies abroad now live among us within the USA.

My time at Quantico went by quickly, and I was getting the itch to go back to 'Nam. Before I could ask for my new orders, an

---

77 Heroes

unexpected set came in for me. I was being sent to Fort Hollibird, Maryland, to the army's intelligence cchool, for fifteen weeks of training.

I was meritoriously promoted to staff sergeant after I finished first in my class of thirty-one at intel school. I loved the counterintelligence training, which now gave me a secondary MOS of 0211. The intelligence MOS also opened new doors that would provide me with valuable inside information about the war. I mused at my becoming a spook.

After the counter-intelligence training, I went TAD[78] to a covert Department of Defense position, where I would help write the book on the crossover knowledge that was shared between snipers and the intelligence community. While it was interesting, there was too much time making up "pretty boards" to brief the brass at the weekly dog-and-pony show. Time was going by at a half-step, and the itch was growing fast.

Months of working from a desk were good for my career, but I began to crave the adrenalin rush I'd get while I was in the field. I had been stateside too long and now it was time for me to return to Vietnam to do the job I was trained to do. I submitted my request for orders back, and they were immediately granted.

In July, a set was placed into the hands of a meritoriously promoted gunnery sergeant. The world maybe wasn't smiling on me, but my Corps, my Marine Corps, certainly was.

The shooting incident at Kent State University, which had left four dead and one seriously wounded, seemed to culminate the ugly, conflicting views of America versus the military. Many of us serving in uniform at this time knew the war was a political football, and that the armed forces were being dictated to, and also run by, civilians. Like it or not, we were doing a job our country called on us

---

[78] Temporary additional duty

to do. We lived in very unsettled times as military men and women in the sixties and seventies.

I wondered once again if I should attempt to contact that now-college-graduate John Fox before being deployed to the land of the dragon once again. Naw, fuck it, I thought. John put all that shit behind him by his own choice, and he was probably knocking down some big bucks as a civilian puke that would deny ever having killed an enemy.

How clever and convenient it was for one country to label another human being with names like gook, slope, dink, gomers, gooners, or zipper-head. Formally, we all knew them as the NVA or VC, but never as the foe that also had a wife, parents, children, and family. That would humanize the enemy too much, and then the euphoric thrill of the hunt and kill would have been diminished.

Our enemy was generally believed by many people to be uneducated and stupid—while in fact, most of the Vietnamese people I knew spoke, read, and wrote anywhere from three to five languages. Underestimate your enemy, and he will bury you and that's for sure. Unfortunately, too many of our most senior officers and politicians underestimated our enemy in Vietnam.

I chose to be a marine and a sniper, and I believed that I was truly professional in all aspects of the job that I'd ask for. There wasn't much to think about when it came right down to it so, Semper Fi, do and die, you bastard, piece-of-shit, slant-eyed gook, fuck-head! With all due respect that is, sir!

The change of view from stateside back to Vietnam now seemed pretty damn good to me, something I had truly looked forward to. I had been in the Land of Oz for way too long, and would you believe that even I was starting to develop a negative attitude?

This time my airplane landed at Ton Son Nhut Airport in Saigon, Republic of Vietnam. I had to go through one week of in-country processing, like I was some sort of a newbie at all of this war stuff. Go figure that some stupid REMF general thought that all of us needed introduction to War 101. *Beaucoup, Dinky Dau Dau Su Dit!*

Da Nang was, in fact, the land of marines while Saigon was the land of the political side of intelligence, generals, and the Emerald City at the end of the mythical yellow brick road.

Or, I suppose, Saigon could also become your last stop before you were embalmed and sent home in a silver box to that stinking free hole in the ground. Even when you were dead, no one ever said welcome home from the war, sailor, soldier, airman, or marine.

Chapter 12

"Good morning, Lieutenant. Gunnery Sergeant McMullin, 1981844 reporting for duty according to my orders, sir."

Because of the covert nature of my orders, they did not even mention the Republic of Vietnam in them. According to this set, I was reporting to Company B, Headquarters Marine Corps, in Washington DC. Sometimes I just had to reflect and smile on some of our shallow and covert attempts at secrecy. Who even gave a shit where I was or where I was going?

"Good morning, Gunny, we were expecting you here around two days ago." I think that I sorta suspected that was coming somehow. I leaned on the desk and motioned for the lieutenant to come closer to me as I began to speak in a hushed voice.

"Yes, sir, well you see, sir, I was actually sidetracked by some cheap-ass whiskey and those Saigon tea whores at MACV. It was because of them that I was both betrayed and delayed, sir! *Xin loi choi oi, beaucoup anh em u lum, co dep lum!*[79] Be still, my palpitating heart!"

This boy-wonder lieutenant had no idea what in the hell I'd just

---

[79] "Sorry about that, *wow*, many beautiful young women loved me too much."

said, but he must have gotten the word about me, because he didn't ask. He looked at me like I'd just been discharged from a funny farm someplace—and, of course, that possibility *did* exist.

This tour, I was attached to Special Operations in Northern I Corps and the DMZ. Because of the clandestine image of this nonexistent command, it appeared that I was there with little or no direct affiliation with any unit or military organization.

In short, I was going to be operating without marines or any other friendlies that knew who or where I was. Generally, I'd be without any communications, so I really was a loose cannon that was out there on my own, so to speak.

This was all well and good to maintain their level of secrecy, but what if I was to get my tit in the wringer? There was little chance anyone could or would ever be able to bail my ass out, so I'd just end up classified as missing in action—someplace that was known only to God, yet denied by my country. Officially, I was really never ever there, wherever in the hell "there" really was.

In a case like that, I would do best just to take myself out rather than to be captured. The word of the day; every day, was to save a .45 round for your own quick demise because these pieces of shit didn't take enlisted men as POWs. Officers were *Ngoc trai*, or *Pearls*, a thing of value to be traded for the special needs of North Vietnam. Enlisted men were disposed of in one to four painful and hideous days—especially if you were a hated *nguoi ban tia*.[80]

Well, as the grunts often said; "They can kill me but they can't eat me!"

I was able to select my own code name and radio call sign this tour. These were literally all I would ever be known by when I was participating in the black or dark side operations.

You know the drill; if I tell you then I have to kill you!

---

[80] Sniper

I chose Ghost Rider.[81] as my code name, because I always liked the song "Ghost Riders in the Sky," sung by Vaughn Monroe in 1949. For my radio call sign, I chose Chime Whiskey.[82]

In theory, someone somewhere knew me and could identify me by either of those two names—the operative words here being "*in theory*"!

Most of the time, I would not take a spotter along with me because of the secrecy attached to the mission. Two men were twice as likely to be compromised as one would be.

Where the hell was Dead Eye Doc when I needed him?

My new rifle was a custom made and custom fitted 7.62 provided by the marine gunsmiths at MCB Quantico. It was a sweet-ass custom-made rifle that was as accurate as any in the world, and it fit me like a well-worn pair of boots—or maybe it was also as comfortable as another treasured and personal part of my body?

My first unofficial/official assignment was to hunt and eliminate a ruthless female sniper and interrogator from the North Vietnamese Army. She had been codenamed Komodo Dragon by the intelligence lads at MACV and the Combined Intelligence Center Vietnam—CICV, or Sick-V as it was pronounced.

Komodo, as she was also known, was very a very fitting code name for this woman, because she was as vicious, cruel, brutal, sadistic, and inhuman as was this almost-prehistoric creature.

Within her own army, she was called, *Nhung phu nu ma tra tan va nhung su giet voi long khao khat.*[83]

The spooks had had tracked this nasty-ass bitch now for some time. It was estimated that she had tortured and killed at least twenty marines in just the past couple of years. When she had the luxury of time, she would take several horrific days and nights making a man

---

81 Nguoi chuoi nguama
82 Ngoc trai ruou
83 The woman that tortures and kills with much lust

cry out for a quick death, just to bring him peace from the suffering that she was dutifully administering.

Her modus operandi was generally close to her trademark. After a man was captured, Komodo would strip him naked and four-point him, meaning she would dislocate his shoulders and hips. After she cut off his eyelids, she would start crushing his fingers and toes and pulling off the nails and tips—one every half-hour. Generally, she would cauterize them with salt so he didn't lose too much blood too soon. Given the time, she would take a hammer or club and break the knees and elbows and any other bones she desired to crush. Teeth were also an object of her attention, especially if a marine had a gold crown. Sometimes she would pull them completely out, but generally they would just be broken at the gum line. She would finish him off by cutting off his penis, sticking it in his mouth, and quickly disemboweling him.

In short, Komodo probably wasn't the ideal woman you wanted to take home to meet your parents. If she actually possessed any semblance of a sane mind, it was about as fucked up as the afterbirth of a primeval gangbang.

The problem with trying to kill Komodo was that she was almost always just a stone's throw from the protection of no less than a full NVA division.

She had been impossible for any of my predecessors to find and to eliminate. To her credit, however, she had killed three of the five American snipers that had gone out hunting for her. They were all found dead and mutilated, as that was her signature warning to any marine seeking to end her blood-splattered and orgasmic interrogations.

During the next five days out in the bush, I followed whom I believed to be Komodo; there were always taunting, tantalizing clues left behind. It wasn't that she actually wanted me to find her; she was baiting me, and I knew exactly what she was doing. War and brutality were just a sick game for this deranged woman who was seemingly, untouchable.

I returned to the base get some decent chow, and then perhaps I'd make a trip to CICV for every possible detail the intel people could provide me on her. I knew and now vowed that somehow, someday, I was going to kill the Komodo Dragon, even if I had to extend my tour in Vietnam to do it. I was becoming as obsessed with my mission of killing as she was with hers. I knew true hate for another human being now, and that became my impetus and drive.

Besides, I had no place better to go and nothing any better to be doing than to get her slimy ass and *cat co hong cua minh.*[84]

Later that week, I was told that the intel lads in Saigon had some credible leads on Komodo. Supposedly, a NVA defector had rolled over on her after his capture. He had provided the people at CDEC[85] with documentation that could conceivably provide me with a route that she was supposed to be using while she was out training new snipers.

The following morning, I was on a C-130 aircraft headed down to Saigon and on to MACV. One of my greatest joys of being in Saigon and Cho Lon was seeing so many of the Vietnamese women who still wore the *ao dai.* This garment was way sexier than a miniskirt, and yet it covered everything but her head.

I had an appointment the next morning at CICV with Army Chief Warrant Officer Kumara. I was told that he knew everything that the US had collected on Komodo, and he could even relate some of her patterns and quirks to me.

---

84 Cut her throat
85 Combined document exploitation center

Chapter 13

I was looking forward to this meeting in the morning, but tonight I was going into town with a marine that was assigned to the US Army 716th Military Police Battalion. We had crossed paths when I was attending my stupid Introduction to War 101. Master Sergeant Ken Adams was a little older than I was, but we came from the same neck of the woods back in Illinois. He came from Collinsville, and I grew up in Belleville. They were both near Edwardsville and Caseyville, none of which warranted a spot on the map. Naturally, we shared the geography and many of good laughs about our antics growing up in the Midwest. He told me that we were going to eat dinner at the Vietnamese Officers Club before venturing out to some of the bars and clubs that he knew about.

The Vietnam Air Force Officers Club was very western and served great American, Vietnamese, and Chinese foods. I was immediately smitten by our waitress; a truly drop-dead beautiful Vietnamese woman named Sarah. Oh my Lord. In truth, the word *smitten* was an understatement; maybe I was more overwhelmed, or perhaps swept off of my feet? This was love at first sight for me. I always thought love that for given any length of time was completely hokey, but this woman was absolutely making my stomach do bigtime flip-flops. I knew full well that Sarah wasn't her real name, and it didn't matter, because it suited her to a tee. *Rat dep lum*!

Ken was trying to be realistic as he chided me, "Perry, do you have any idea how many men have hit on her and tried to get just a date? You look like a high-school kid when you grin at her, but if you'd like, I'll introduce you to her later. She gets off of work here pretty soon. Of course, she'll tell you there is no way, because she always tells every American that hits on her, '*No way!*' This is just a fair warning to you, because I don't want to see you get a broken heart and spend the rest of the night tripping over your pouting bottom lip!"

"Thanks, Ken, but just introduce us and leave it at that, okay?"

Sarah was indeed as beautiful and as lithe as a cat. I simply could not take my eyes off of her, and I'm sure that was obvious to her also. The *ao dai* she was wearing was a deep purple over bright-yellow pants, and it fit her perfectly, complementing her small but amazing body. Sarah was about five foot, six inches tall with black, silky hair that went to her waist. She was incredibly beautiful, but it was her eyes that captured and held me. There was just something about them—and her—that completely blew me away. Outstanding, outstanding, outstanding!

When Sarah ceremoniously asked us if there would be anything else for our dinner, Ken said, "Gunny McMullin wants to know if you would join us for a drink here at the club, and then maybe you and I can show him around Saigon before he has to go back up north in two or three days."

Sarah kept her head slightly bowed, but those gorgeous, black, and almond eyes flashed over to mine as she shook her head no and smiled at me. "Thank you both so very much, but I must catch a taxi home from here, and the driver is my brother. He gets very worried if he cannot take me home from work. My brother was badly wounded while he was in the army, so now he drives a taxi to help support our family."

I nodded my head to acknowledge what she said. Sarah's English was good, very good, but in the typical Asian custom, she hesitated to make direct eye contact when the conversation was light and not of a personal nature. I stood up and took her hand—well actually her fingers—in mine. With that, she again made direct eye contact with me. *"Sarah, hay yeu cau anh trai cau ban de div au cui lac bo va chaise mot thuc uong voi chung toi neu anh ta se. Sau do ong co the duoc lai xe cah chung toi cho phan con lai cua dem. Toi se tra gap doi so tien anh ta neu anh ta se."*[86]

Ken snapped his head toward me as I spoke to her. "Holy shit, Perry, you sound just like one of them," Ken nearly shouted. "You didn't tell me that you spoke Vietnamese."

Sarah smiled at me and touched my shoulder as she began to walk away from us, but she made eye contact once again. However, this time, I believed that her smile was more than just being professional or nice. This smile was warm and genuinely just for me.

"Cam on ban rang ong. Toi se den va moi anh em anh em cua toi de chia se thoi gian voi chung toi. Xn vui long noi tieng ang voi ca hai chung toi de cua ban se cua ban la Perry rat tot."[87]

"Where in the hell did that come from, Perry?" Ken said. "What, are you some kind of a spook or something? Fuck me hard, Gunny, you speak Vietnamese just like one of those damn gooners is talking."

"First of all, Master Sergeant, please don't disrespect the Vietnamese. Remember, it was you that didn't understand what we said because you are limited to just the one language. I probably could have spoken to her in French, Cambodian, Laos, Chinese, or Japanese.

---

[86] "Sarah, please ask your brother to come into the club and share a drink with us, if he will. Then he can be our driver for the rest of the night if he is willing. I will pay him double the amount if he will go with us."

[87] "Thank you, sir. I will go and invite my brother to share time with us. Please speak English with both of us, so your friend won't feel left out. Your Vietnamese is very good, Perry."

"Besides, I am going to marry her, and she will be the mother of my children!"

Ken smiled at my comment and raised his drink to toast both Sarah and me. "Considering that she has never been known to date any American, that whole marriage concept will come as a complete surprise to her, I'm quite sure of that." His smirk pissed me off, but, at this moment, it was Sarah who had my undivided attention.

She soon returned to our table with her brother. She had to finish up with a few things, so Ken and I sat and talked with him. I'm sure he noticed that my eyes kept following his sister's every move. But I think that he was also impressed with my Vietnamese.

The backseat of his small taxicab was cramped for two people, so Sarah and I could not help but make unintentional body contact. Sarah's hand was resting on her knee when I put my hand on hers. At first I could feel her begin to pull it away, but then she returned it and began rubbing my fingers with her own. After a moment, I chanced a glance at her. Sarah was smiling as her incredible black eyes met mine and held there. I don't remember where that taxi ride took us or anything her tour-guide brother spoke about that evening. I just know that my heart was pounding like a drum the entire time.

The following morning, I had to get down to the business at hand. I met with Chief Warrant Officer Kumara and Doi Truong[88] Bong. They enlightened me with everything they knew of *Nhung phu ma tra tan va nhung su giet voi long khao khat.* I listened to them and I tried hard to keep my mind strictly on the subject of Komodo. We went over page after page after page of time-consuming information that filled and began to overfloweth my lame attempt to pay attention. Indeed, my mind was slipping away to tonight and my unchaperoned evening with Sarah.

My supposedly short trip to Saigon turned into an extraordinary

---

[88] Captain

eight days. You know, this business of military intelligence is a very, very, very complicated affair that requires deep thought and total thoroughness without interruption. At least that was the bullshit story I told them back at Da Nang. I called and spoke with the colonel, explaining the need for me to extend my stay in Saigon. He was cool and asked me how long I planned to be detained there. He also knew damn good and well that my business at CICV was concluded.

In reality, I had completed my meeting with CWO Kumara and Doi Truong Bong that very same day. I still needed thinking time to decipher everything I had learned while Sarah and I spent the next four days together at the beach in Cam Rahn Bay. Sarah never asked me what the nature of my business was in Saigon, and I think she knew that I'd have to lie to her if I said anything. Our time together was all about two people, and not about the war.

I had two days left to be with her, and that time was glorious, to say the least. For once, I wished that I didn't have to go back to the matter of war, my job, the base, or, for that matter, the Marines. I was trying to figure out something that would allow us to stay together, when a perfect idea came to me.

"Sarah, would you marry me today, right now?" I blurted out. "I love you very much, Sarah, and our different lives do not matter at all. I know that I am the only man you have ever been with, and you are not just a one-night stand. I just want to spend the rest of my life with you."

I'm not sure who was the most shocked by those words—Sarah who was hearing them from me, or myself, who was actually saying the words to her. She studied my face for a moment, and then a beautiful smile grew on her mouth until she nodded her head her head yes and whispered, "Yes, my blue-eyed marine; I will marry you. *Anh yeu em qua.*"[89]

---

[89] "I love you too."

We were married within the hour by a priest at the Catholic church in Saigon, the one that has the two large steeples that can be seen from as far away as the Chinese city of Cholon.

Now I would have to beat feet over to the American Embassy and start the volumes of paperwork that would be necessary for us make our marriage USA-legal. I knew this was going to be an uphill battle with my security clearance, but I didn't think that they could tell me no. It would probably take my entire one-year tour for us to get it done, and I would extend if it came to that.

Leaving her the next day was the hardest thing I had ever done in my life. I knew that I could get hops[90] down and back easily with all of the air traffic that went back and forth.

"I'll be back to Saigon in a few weeks," I told her.

I would just do my time in the bush, and then I'd have to come back down to headquarters to fill the intel lads in on what I had seen and done.

As I was holding her against my chest, she began to cry, and then that was all it took for me too. A hardcore marine became reduced to a blubbering idiot right there in front of God and everybody. The Marine Corps had become my entire life before Sarah married me, and now there was her—mostly her. I could smell her hair and feel the silkiness of it as my tears flowed with hers. She was my wife and my reason to love and to live from now on. Love and hate are both strong emotions, but I believe that love was the stronger of the two.

The ride back to Da Nang seemed extra long that morning, and I kept hearing the song from the movie, *Love is a Many Splendored Thing*, going round and round in my head. I hated that movie when I saw it as a kid back in 1955, but now I imagined watching it with Sarah.

---

90 Flights

Chapter 14

After going over the sketchy information with my colonel and studying the newest aerial photographs of Komodo's suspected route, we decided it was worth the gamble to try and get her. I opted out on a spotter going with me, because of the time I would have to lie in wait on the jungle trail, and, quite frankly, I didn't want the excess baggage or the company. Given the choice, I preferred to work alone; and, generally, I was given that choice.

*   *   *

I would be taken part of the way in by chopper, and then I'd rappel down to my initial starting point. From there I would have to move cautiously for another ten kilometers, in hopes of finding the trail that she would reportedly be using. It was a seldom-used trail and almost impossible to see from the aerial photographs. If we had been given straight scoop, I would find her moving north on this trail with about five or six trainees.

At best the information we had obtained was fifty-fifty. Factoring in the luck of being at the right place, at the right time, on the right trail was making this objective pretty slim. But, because of the high priority of her capture or kill, it was too damn good to pass on any chance of my getting her, slim or not.

Once I was in the dense jungle, I laid low, waiting to insure that the gooners hadn't seen or heard me dropping in. I laid there motionless, with ants crawling over me, stinging and biting and raising welts under the thick ghillie suit. These little bastards made being still nearly impossible, until complete darkness gave me the opportunity to move out with them still gnawing away. At last, I was able to roll over a few times, squashing some of them. If I could find some water to lie in, they would either drown or choose to abandon ship—or sniper, as the case may be.

This area was totally owned by the NVA, so I had to take great care to proceed slowly and avoid being compromised. In order to move forward at the same pace as the wind would move the grass or brush, you had to be very in tune with your immediate environment.

As I was crawling toward a small river, I heard a noise just ahead of me and off to my right. I stopped immediately, lying there completely motionless, listening. It was pitch dark, so nothing could be seen. When one of your senses is disabled, another will become more sensitive. This being the case, it seemed like I had Superman's hearing.

It didn't sound like human noise, because there was a sort of low rumbling that was almost inaudible. It was something that I could almost feel rather than hear. What I finally decided I listening to was meat being chewed and pulled from a carcass. Occasionally, there was the snap of a bone breaking or flesh being torn and eaten.

After laying there for at least an hour, I confirmed to myself that, indeed, this was a *con ho*[91] eating his kill. This created a huge problem in my timing to make it to point alpha where I had hoped to set up and lie low for my target to appear. If I tried to move an inch and the tiger was to catch my scent or hear any noise, he would

---

[91] Tiger

most likely come to investigate rather than run away. No doubt, he would protect his kill at any and all cost to him. Obviously, the tiger had not noticed me, because it continued tearing at the meat and chuffing like one happy feral cat.

Hopefully, now it would get its fill and mosey away to its den or someplace else. An encounter with a full-grown tiger would not only give away my position, but, if a gunshot became necessary to defend myself, I'd still be screwed. I took my KA-Bar from the sheath, but only for use as a last resort. Knife versus tiger were not the kind of odds that I liked right now. Even that struggle would be heard by the enemy, and I'd be burned, so, at this point, all I could do was to wait the tiger out.

Daylight came, and I could still hear some slight movement. I think it had napped, eaten some more, and was now it was just taking it easy; chuffing away. I was already past my turnaround time, because my window of opportunity would have closed by now. The mission was a scrub.

It looked as if Komodo had skated by once more. As slim as my odds may have been, I at least had chance to put my crosshairs on her slimy-ass body. I knew she wasn't as charmed or magical as her reputation with many Asians made it out to be. My diligence would win over her arrogance.

I didn't want to travel during daylight very much, so I decided to wait it out and see if there was still an opportunity when tiger playtime was over. About an hour later, the big cat ambled away from the food, and I figured it was going for water. This was my chance to turn and move far enough away to be safe from the big cat. I would then just hunker down until dark, when I could move out again for my pick-up location to go back home.

I made contact with my ride, and I chanced running into an open LZ, rather than them trying to drop the penetrator into the jungle and pull me up through the trees. There was more risk with an open-field landing, but there was just me, and at least they didn't have to hover. There was risk for them and for me either, way but I was starting to swell from the ant bites and stings, so I went with the quicker option tonight.

Of course, I was disappointed in the results of this mission, but who knows? Maybe that tiger was some sort of an omen either to or for me? I wondered if maybe this was the Asian year of the *con ho*?

Chapter 15

I was lying on my rack, just kicking back and smoking a piss-poor excuse for a cigar and thinking of my wife when some boot PFC came knocking on the hatch of my hardback tent. *Bang, bang, bang!* Three knocks—just the way we had been taught to knock while in boot camp. He nervously informed me that my presence was "required" at the chapel, post haste.

"*The chapel?*" I questioned. "Who in the hell wants to see me over at the chapel and why?"

This kid was as nervous as his first day in boot camp. All he wanted to do was to deliver the message without conversing with me and haul his ass back to the duty hut. His voice squeaked as he replied, "I don't know, sir. They just told me to come and tell you."

I flipped my cigar past his head and out the door of my tent. "Don't call me, sir, you dipshit, because I'm *not* an officer! Oh, for God's sake, never mind ... carry on!"

The only reason I even knew where the chapel was is because I'd pass it on my way to the staff NCO club to get drunk whenever possible.

This must be some stupid, top-secret, bullshit thing going on I imagined. No, that couldn't be the answer either, because no one would ever do a briefing or some other dog-and-pony show at the chapel.

I wondered what in the hell was going on here.

It was too damn hot to wear anything but my green skivvies, but I pulled my trousers and boots on to walk over to the chapel. This just didn't make any sense to me at all.

The chapel was located in a Quonset hut, and it felt a bit cooler inside than the burning, hot-ass sun was outside. I walked through the hatch and toward an officer who was dressed in his tidy, white, navy officer's uniform.

He was standing with his back to me, but as I approached him at the altar, he shouted, "*Zaaaapper!*

What? My mind was reeling. Who the hell was this that knew me by my first-tour tag-name of Zapper? I didn't think anyone knew me by that name anymore.

The man unexpectedly turned around, sticking his hand out toward me, grinning ear to ear.

"Dead Eye Doc?" I said. "John Fox? No shit; John Fox?" This wasn't coming together for me at all. "What the fuck is going on here?" I stammered.

"Hey, hey, now, Gunny. Is that any way for you to address a navy officer, and, for sure, a navy chaplain? Ya know, Zapper, I always knew you were a bit of a crude leatherneck, but please, be respectful while you are here in my church. I'm not too sure if you could ever manage that, but please try real hard for me."

I couldn't speak. Fox or Doc or someone that looked just like him was actually standing right there in front of me, all dressed up in a spiffy navy officer's uniform. The kicker was that he was also wearing the cross of a chaplain on his shoulder boards.

"Please sit down, Perry, before I have to pour some communion wine in your wide-open mouth. We have some catching up to do, I suppose?"

I still couldn't put this together. "Okay, wait a minute. Is this on the level, Doc? I mean you are John Henry Fox, the Dead Eye Doc corpsman from a few years ago? You just gotta be shit'n me, John; I mean, what the hell is going on here?"

He just sat there, grinning ear to ear, and I knew that he was enjoying each and every moment of my confusion. "I'll tell you what, Gunny, let's go to the O-club for some warm tiger piss, and I'll fill you in on the scoop. I'm pretty sure that it is my turn to buy today too."

A couple of things had changed considerably since our last tour together. The club was now larger, and the semiavailable US beer was not cold—but it wasn't hot either. What had changed was the obvious, and here he was, sitting and talking to me like we were waiting for the freedom bird to take us home some time ago.

John sat down and began to fill me in on what he had been doing while he was away at college.

"I sort of got out of the navy, and I went off to college, like I said I was going to do. You remember when I said I wanted to be a chaplain's assistant and not a corpsman when we first met? Well, I became a Baptist minister, but I remained in the Navy ROTC program during my years in college. I was commissioned as an officer, and I really felt my calling was back here in Vietnam. Some quaint little white church with a cute little picket fence around it to keep the cows from mooing during my Sunday sermon just wasn't my dream. I wouldn't want to put everyone to sleep, you know.

"I checked in with Headquarters Marine Corps, and I discovered that you were back in country, so I asked to come and see if I could woo you into attending my Sunday services, you pagan marine lifer.

"So now you are up to snuff on me, what are you doing here again? Are you still doing the one-shot, one-kill sniper thing? You have done very well in rank too, Zapper; a gunny already? I'm impressed."

"I'm still in shock at seeing you, Doc. I guess I should say, 'Your Ensignship' or 'chaplain' or 'Your Holiness' or something like that? Of course, John, I am still a sniper, but I also carry an intel MOS as my secondary and did a tour at DOD and NIS.

"Snipers are better trained now, and we have become more sophisticated than we were when you first spotted for me. I am supporting Special Tactical Operations this time in 'Nam, and so, consequently, if I tell you anything I'll just have to kill you. But then, killing a navy officer—and a chaplain to boot—well, that would make my future home at Portsmouth Naval Prison, wouldn't it?

"Seriously, my friend, I am deeply covert, and so I'm not at liberty to say anything about what or when I do things. In fact, what I'm doing is so secret, I'm not allowed to even talk to myself. You know the drill."

He said, "Yeah, I do, Zapper. I thought about becoming a navy doctor, but then I just really felt a calling to wear the cross of a chaplain." John chuckled when he said, "I guess that we—that is, you and I—are still a team of sorts, Gunny. We may not be the same kind of team we were once before, Gunny, but now I'd say that our team is more like *the cross and the sword.*

"Strange the way things turn out, the way our lives go? I don't want to stay here on base preaching Sunday services, because I want to go out in the field and be with the grunts. I miss our time in the field together, but not the killing aspect of what we did once before."

After a couple of beers, Doc or the chaplain said he wanted to unpack and get into some more comfortable cammies. I wondered how long it would take me to get used to stop calling this new navy ensign "Doc." I was going to fill him in on my marriage to Sarah, but there would be ample time to do that later on, and I wanted to show him pictures of her when I gave him the fantastic news.

*   *   *

I got back to my tent, and I was rummaging through my footlocker for another cheap Red Dot or Crooks Rum River cigar to smoke and gnaw on.

That same boot PFC that had summoned me before came back again. "Excuse me, sir. You are wanted at the Special Tactical Operations CP, right away."

"Damn it, Marine, will you please quit calling me *sir*! Do I look like a college graduate or an officer to you? I am a gunnery sergeant in the United States Marine Corps, so quit calling me sir, okay? If I walk as a duck and I quack like a duck, then I must be a fucking duck—but I don't quack you dumb ass, so I am neither an officer nor a duck … for that matter! Okay, as you were, Private. Go and smoke this cigar, because it might put a hair on your skinny-ass chest!"

The Special Tactical Operations CP was located within a secure enclosure, guarded by a machine gun tower and two guards at the outer barb wire entry. Even though the sentries on duty knew full well who I was, I still had to return to my tent for my military identification card that was stashed away in my footlocker. Even General Westmoreland would have to do the same thing, so I knew I wasn't exempt. It was just an annoyance to walk back and forth, because I might be tempted to impersonate myself as myself.

"*Xin chao dai ta, Vargas. Mot cai gi do lon phai duoc xay ra?*"[92]

The colonel replied, "*Xui chao, Gunny. Hay lay mot cai ghe.*"[93]

"Gunny, we have a mission of enormous consequence, and, of course, it is classified all of the way to the very highest level. The spooks have found an NVA POW camp that is surprisingly not all that far from us. This camp is located just out of country, and intel

---

[92] "Good afternoon, Colonel Vargas. Something big must be going on."
[93] "Hello, Gunny, please take a chair."

has it that there are three American pilots that are being held there until they can be moved up north. Of course, that makes the timing very critical for us. And that's not all—there is another problem. One of the pilots is a navy commander that has worked with some very critical and classified information. That man cannot, under any circumstances, be allowed to fall into the hands of the enemy interrogators. Why in the hell the US Navy ever let him fly a combat mission into Laos is way beyond me, but they did, and he was shot down. Now it falls back on us to clean up this shitty mess that they've created. Therefore, in two days, *muoi*[94] Marine Force Recon and Navy SEAL team members will attack this POW camp to extract the three pilots. You will be providing the supporting sniper fire from a completely different location. In fact, it is pretty far away from all of our other people. They can't come help you if you get your tit in a wringer, so as usual, Ghost Rider … you are out there on your own again. It is imperative that you take out both of the NVA soldiers that are located in a makeshift machine-gun tower on the northwest corner of the camp. Gunny, if you don't take them out, the mission will fail, and our men will be hammered by the heavy machinegun fire. They have to be taken out for this mission either to begin, or to ultimately succeed. That can't be said or stressed too much, because you and you alone are the key element."

Colonel Vargas stopped speaking to get a drink of water. When he came back, he sat and studied me for a moment. "Now here is the really grungy part of this mission. Neh chung toi khong than cong trong viec nay noi rieng. *Ban se phai trung hoa ong ta truoc khi ong ta co the duoc chuyen len phia bac cho su tham van boi quan doi.*[95]

"You will have about an eight-hundred meter shot either way,

---

94 "Ten"
95 "Should we not succeed in the recovery of this particular officer, you will have to neutralize him before he can be moved up north for interrogation by their army."

but one of these two scenarios must and will play out. He comes out alive and back in our hands or …

"*Ban hieu chat day du va tam quan trong cua nhiem va nay nay gunny? Dieu nay vuot xabi mat hang dau.*"[96]

I replied, "*Chi can nhung gi ma fuck la ban che toi o day dai ta? Toi la mot sniper bien toi khong phai la mot sat thu va do la chinh xac nhung gi tol dang duoc noi o day tro thanh.*"[97]

"What if the sentries in the tower can't be taken out, sir? Will the SEALs still attack the camp? Will they still attempt the rescue? This is really a cluster fuck mission that sounds to me like there is just a one way ticket available."

He just sat there eyeballing me for a moment. "*Toi biet rang no hut,*[98] Gunny, but if the two men in that tower are not killed outright, those ten SEALs that are attempting to breech that gate will be cut to ribbons. By then, we will have then lost all of the elements that are necessary to allow us to make this rescue. If this attack scrubs, that man cannot be allowed to be moved from that camp by the enemy. Now if that makes you a *thich khach,*[99] then so be it. We both will still follow our orders as they are given to us, won't we now, Gunnery Sergeant McMullin?" There was a long pause as the colonel sat there and eyeballed me hard once again.

Colonel Jay Vargas was the best Marine Corps colonel I knew; he was respected as an officer and as a leader. Colonel Vargas had been a grunt officer, so he'd done his time in hell. Every marine under his command would follow him to capture the devil himself.

---

[96] "Do you understand the full nature and the significance of this mission, Gunny? This mission goes well beyond top secret."

[97] "Just what the fuck are you telling me here, Colonel Vargas? I am a marine sniper, I'm not an assassin, and that is exactly what I am being told to become."

[98] "I know it sucks."

[99] "Assassin"

I respected him to the max, but I certainly didn't like the message he was sending to me at this moment.

"So, if I have made myself perfectly clear, those are in fact your orders, Gunny, and you will be briefed tomorrow with a mockup of the POW camp. I'll see you at the intelligence briefing promptly at zero eight hundred."

As I stood to leave, Colonel Vargas said, "Oh, and by the way, Gunny, you will be taking a spotter along with you this time. You will need another person to give you the range and the windage very quickly. Two shots fired and two enemy dead are absolutely imperative, so we can't afford a miss in either of the two cases. For the sake of speed and accuracy and because another set of eyes are imperative, *you will take a spotter along with you.*

"Unfortunately, the only man who has a top-secret clearance that can make the mission with you is just out of school, and he has never been on a combat mission before."

"Oi choi oi, Colonel Vargas. I can't take a FNG out on a mission like this. You people are stacking the frigg'n deck against me, and against the lives of every man out there. I'd rather go it alone than to have some kid fall apart when I need him the most. We have no idea what we will be facing out there."

About all there was left to say to completely ruin my day was for someone to tell me to stand at attention so I could be delivered a knee-drive in the nuts. I was thinking that the best thing for me to do was to shut up and just nod my head, even though that usually went against my grain.

"PFC Bogdan will be here at the briefing tomorrow, Gunny. I don't like this thing that we are faced with either, Perry, but goddamn it; you know as well as I do that this comes from higher places, and you and I are not in the loop to just do what we think would be best. I'll see you here tomorrow at 0800.

"*O day mot cigar phong nha cho su thay doi va sau do co duoc cho*

minh mot so giac ngu ban muon tot khong lien ket voi jack cho cac cap
vo chong tiep theo cua ngay."[100]

Yeah, right, get some sleep, the colonel said. He just told me that I'm the success or the failure of this entire mission and that the lives of thirteen or more Americans will depend on me. Oh sure, I'll just mosey my grunt ass back to that sweltering shithole tent and plop myself down for a good night's sleep without a frigg'n care in the world.

I opened up my footlocker and I took out a full bottle of Jack Daniels Black Label and another one of my cigars to smoke and chew. I'd save the colonel's expensive three-dollar stateside stogie to smoke—if and when I come back from this mission.

About halfway through the bottle of Jack Daniel's, I laid back and smiled. "Yea, though I walk through the valley of the shadow of death, I will fear no evil." At this point, I was feeling pretty sorry for myself, and I missed my wife.

The Jack Daniels and the sleeping pills were kicking my ass, so I would rest well tonight in spite of the clusterfuck mission that was waiting for me the day after tomorrow.

"Gunny! *Hey, Gunny!* They want you at the CP about five minutes ago. Come on, Gunny, the colonel said for you to get yer ass over there right away, so double-time!"

"Yeah, yeah, YEAH! Christ almighty! Give me a fucking break! I'm on my way over there so just go … carry on … PLEASE!"

The sun was extra bright from my hangover as I walked toward the CP. Maybe they moved the POWs last night, and so it would be too late for a rescue attempt. Maybe the fucking intelligence people decided just to kill everyone with a cluster bomb. Maybe if pigs had wings they could fly up Washington DC's brass asshole. I was not a happy camper this morning!

---

[100] "Here have a decent cigar for a change and then get yourself some sleep. You'd best not associate with Mister Jack for the next couple of days."

As I got close to the armed guards at the entryway a boy wearing a marine uniform came running full speed right at me. When he was right up in my face, he hit the brakes, kicking up a cloud of dust that enveloped me. I had a hangover, I didn't have any coffee yet, and my sleeping pills had left my mouth tasting like the entire Communist Chinese Army had marched through it with dirty boots. A boy that looked all of sixteen years old acted like he had been summoned by his Boy Scout leader to earn a merit badge for top-secret missions today.

"Good morning, Gunny McMullin. I'm PFC Bogdan and I'm told that I am to be your new spotter." My hangover wasn't helping him, or me, at this point.

"Bogdan? Do you even shave yet, lad? I bet you know the entire Marine Corps Hymn word for word too, don't you? Go earn your goddamn Combat Action Ribbon someplace else there, PFC Bogdan, because there ain't a chance in hell that you are going to earn it while you are with me." I didn't like him, his look, his pimples, or his childish behavior. He would ruin the mission before he got to the POW camp. I walked away from PFC Bogdan, mumbling, *"Xin loi ve dieu do ban nguoi ngu ngoc gay la con cho tham tu."*[101]

There was nothing that had changed from what the colonel told me yesterday. I looked at the model of the temporary POW camp. It was small, with two grass-and-bamboo huts located in the center of the bamboo and barbed wire outer walls.

The tower in question was not very big—maybe six feet off the ground and about five feet by five feet square. Although it was put together in a hurry, it commanded the approach and gave a full three-sixty of the small camp. Supposedly, there were always two men in the tower, which sported a heavy machine gun that made any approach toward the compound impossible. The two soldiers there would have also had their AK-47s, and we guessed that there

---

[101] "So sorry about that, you stupid-looking, broke-dick dog."

was a scattering of buried landmines surrounding the compound too. Aerial photography led us to believe that there were only a dozen or less NVA soldiers guarding the three Americans, so that was a real ray of sunshine coming through the gloom and doom of this mission.

Obviously, the guards in the tower were the key to the success of the operation, and they were mine and mine alone to neutralize.

There was a ridge off to the south of the camp; it was about two hundred feet higher than the tower was. Without the surrounding jungle, I would generally have an easy thousand-meter shot, but with all of the vegetation out there, who could tell?

Maybe it was a shot that could be made and maybe it wasn't. There was no way of knowing that from the ancient topographic, one-to-fifty-thousand map that was probably not even marginally close to being accurate. There were just too many goddamn if, if, *if's* that were still in place here. Questions without answers and problems without solutions was all I could see looming in front of me.

Most of all, I did not want to take this boy marine along with me. Now was told that, in addition to all the other di tieu[102] that is being heaped on me, I was supposed to provide daycare for some pogey bait-eating, pimply faced, untested, immature, titty-sucking kid!

As the briefing began to break up, Colonel Vargas motioned me to cool my jets and to hang back with him. Before I could start to conjure up scenarios, he walked over close to me and waited for the last person to leave the room. "Look, Gunny Mac, I know that this mission has a high-risk price-tag attached to it, and I'd like for you to have at least twenty-four hours in Saigon with your wife, Sarah. Unfortunately time won't allow for that, and I probably couldn't allow the visit anyway now that you have been briefed and all."

I was generally pretty well known for my poker-face, but he

---

102 Shit.

caught me off guard with this tidbit of knowledge, because I hadn't disclosed our marriage to anyone up here. As I started to speak, he just grinned and held up his hand. "Here, you can have this picture of her from the club, because I have plenty more. Ya know, Gunny, it is our job to know secrets, but not to be a part of one. Congratulations are in order, and, trust me, she is already being investigated. We'll chat more about this matter when you come back. Carry on, ol' married man!"

Unfortunately, my trip back to see Sarah would be on hold for a while. The thoughts of the warm, sandy beaches at Vung Tau and Sarah seemed so close, but so far away from me right now. It would have been nice to be able to close my eyes for a while, just to daydream of her. I had been able to make a couple of phone calls, and I had written a letter, but I missed being with her more than I've missed anyone in my life. Good Lord! Sarah is my wife—I was actually *ket hon*![103]

---

[103] Married

Chapter 16

I was proned out my rack, wearing only my skivvies as I tried my best to endure the stifling, muggy heat that was inside the tent from hell. As if it wasn't bad enough inside my green sauna-like tent, some butthead was pounding on the hatch to come in and pester me again. "Oh, for God's sake," I mumbled aloud. It couldn't possibly be that same damn runner coming back here and calling me *sir* again, could it?

"WHAT ... in ... the ... HELL do you want this time?" I snarled toward the door as I clenched my badly mauled cigar between my teeth.

Ensign Fox cautiously stuck his head inside the tent and said, "It sounds like you may be having a down day, Gunny." He was looking around for another person, or at least a source for my bad mind-set, I supposed.

"*Xuong ngay?*[104] Padre, you have absolutely no clue just how deep the river runs right now. A down day would be a colossal simplification of what is going on in my word right now. First, the Marine Corps wants me to do the impossible mission. Furthermore,

---

[104] Down day

they have hung this entire screwed-up mess around my neck with a frick'n battleship anchor attached. I'm not sure that even you could pull this abortion-destined cluster-fuck off, and that is with all of those magnificent contacts you have obtained in that big headquarters up yonder." I was pointing up at the top of the tent, but I think that he still got the idea.

"Ah, but Gunny, you should never underestimate the power of the Lord and prayer."

I rubbed my alcohol-blurred, hungover, tortured eyes as I heaved a frustrated, deep sigh. "Maybe if the Lord would like to come along with me on this particular mission tomorrow, we might pull this thing off while working together. However, unless the Lord is a better spotter than you were, I am still up the old cluster-fuck creek without a serviceable paddle. Unfortunately, so are maybe thirteen other Americans that will also be doomed if I fail.

"And I'm not done yet either, my friend. Not only do I have this shithole of a situation to manage, but they also have ordered me to take along some FNG, boy blunder, wannabe spotter that has never even had a hostile shot fired toward him. The brass assholes have decided in their infinite wisdom that he absolutely must come along with me into the valley of death. I'd much rather go this whole thing alone, but they gave me zero, zippo, frigg'n nada choice in the entire matter, and that comes down to me in the form of a direct order. Aside from that, my day is just splendid, and thanks for asking, Chaplain."

John sat on my footlocker, looking intently at me, but not speaking for a minute. "So, tell me something, Gunny—does all of this come down to your not needing him or is it that you don't want this particular spotter to go along with you because he is a newbie? Is it this spotter situation alone that is making this entire mission so completely impossible?"

"No, *Vi cha dao*,[105] it doesn't all come down to the spotter thing, but if this kid freaks out when bullets start to fly, he'll jeopardize not only my entire mission, but also the lives of every man out there—including his and mine."

I actually did see the need for a spotter to give me necessary, quick, and precise information for that first and second quick kill shot. I still thought that I'd be better off going it alone than taking this John Wayne wannabe along with me. "He is already scared shitless, and he hasn't even broken the stateside starched crease in his newly issued uniform yet. He personifies FNG!"

John pondered my comments, and then he said, "It sounds pretty darn crucial to me too, Gunny, and I never knew of you to sweat the small stuff—or even the bigger stuff for that matter. So why is whoever they are so dead set on this kid going along if he can't do the job? There has to be some other seasoned spotters that you could be taking along with you?"

I said, "Yeah, there are, but given the uniqueness, secrecy, and the covert nature of this special mission, it requires a top-secret security clearance. Due to so many recent stateside rotations slamming us, it only leaves this boy blunder as the one and the only that possesses that particular piece of magical paper. I don't know—one stinking security clearance may very well cost both me and some Navy SEALs their lives. All of that adds up to this sucking a big, fat *hachi*! Oh, and it even gets way worse and much deeper than what I've told you already, Doc. There are other American lives at stake here too, so I guess the body count could reach fifteen or more should this mission piss backward on me."

John now sat and contemplated the situation once again. He knew this one had me stumped, and that it was lacking any forward direction at all. He intently studied an ugly green bug on the floor

---

105 Padre

and finally shook his head before he looked up at me with a grin on his face. "Gunny Mac, did you just offer me a shot of Jack Daniel's? If you didn't, please be polite enough to pour each of us a shot anyway." As he stood up to take the water glass that was one-fourth full of whiskey, he moved close enough to viciously stomp the insect. "That bug looked like the devil," he said, still grinning.

After we downed a couple more straight-ups, John got back to business. "Well, I can see that this is a highly classified and difficult mission, Perry, and I'm just thinking about something that is sorta way out there. You see, I still have my top-secret clearance, and I'm quite sure that I can still spot right along with the best of the seasoned spotters. You don't have to compromise the nature of this mission to me because you and I both know that I don't have the need to know. However, according to navy regs, I can still go anyplace in country, be it a combat zone or Saigon. I have a couple of days before I have to write my Sunday sermon, so why don't you just ditch this new guy and take me along with you? We were once a great team; we were in fact the best team that ever existed, and we will always remain a team of sorts, Zapper."

Oi choi oi. I almost bit my brand new cigar in half when Doc said for me to take him along with me. "What am I supposed to do now, laugh?" I smiled. "Come on, John. It has been umpteen years since we have seen or even worked together as a team. You know it isn't about me being concerned with your skills, because you are a natural, and I know you still have the knack. But let's just take a real close look at the uniform you have on, and then at your rank. See if you can tell then me straight up that you could still go out and do this mission. We'd both be hung by our necks—or maybe something even shorter and worse if we even attempted to pull off this 'cross and the sword' thing, Doc."

John now got that same old intense look of determination within his eyes that the old corpsman I used to know would get. "What can anyone do to us, Gunny? It isn't like they can shave our heads and send us off to Vietnam, right? There are absolutely no regulations that prohibit an officer from being in combat, be they marine or navy. There are many officers serving in the field as we speak. I have both the skill, and I have the necessary clearance to go out with you, while that private doesn't."

Okay, he'd made a good point there, and that took some of the wind out of my sails. "Look Fox, you're not a corpsman anymore; you are a United States Navy Chaplain and an officer. Strike one, strike two, and strike three—yer out!"

"So what, Gunny? You can't tell me that you have never seen a chaplain out in the field. I'd generally try to save their souls, but if I can save their lives first, then I'll have more time to work on that whole soul issue later on. Chaplains have been killed in every war, so this isn't all that unreasonable."

I guess he had me beat there again, but there was still one major—or make that a full bird colonel—obstacle.

"Okay, look, I'm good to go with this so far, Chaplain John Henry Fox, but how in the hell do we convince the old man? The CO will never ever buy into this debacle, and he'd throw our asses out of the command post if we even tried to approach him with it. And you can't say 'don't tell him that we switched spotters,' because he'd really be pissed when he found out. I know we are both really and truly invincible, but suppose—just suppose for one lousy, frigg'n moment—that you get zapped out there?

"Nope there's no way, Jose. If I'd even tried to present this to the old man, I already know exactly what he'd say. He'd say how many *R*s are there in fat chance, Gunny?"

The chaplain didn't even flinch when he responded; in fact, John actually laughed at me. "Look, if I should get killed, I'll have no part in knowing how your court martial turns out, will I? But then, if you get killed, I will simply say that you'd kidnapped me and you made me go along with you." John was dead serious about the topic at hand, but his delivery speech was putting that old spark I used to see back in his eyes. "So, how and where do we go from here? I suspect we have a lot of work to do in an increasingly short amount of time."

"Okay, okay. Once again, you have made your point, and a very strong argument as well. There is just one more, teeny, tiny, itsy, bitsy other thing you maybe should know about—this is a mission that probably will not succeed at all, Preacher John; in fact, it has all of the earmarks of a suicide mission from the very get-go. Look—number one, this mission will take us into a hornets' nest of the *Bo Doi.*[106]

"Secondly, we won't have any kind of communications with us, and that's for several different reasons.

"Thirdly, if we do miss our preset time for pick-up, we will have to hump our way back through Indian country to Firebase Davis, because they won't fly back in for us.

"And then, lastly, my friend, you know what the *Bo Doi* will do to us if, in fact, we are captured. As you well know, we as snipers don't exactly make their top-ten list of high society. Our death will be certain and it will be … slow. They will treat us worse than the *cong khi*[107] they've killed and are fixing to eat for dinner later on. Now, if that doesn't change yer cotton-pickin' mind, you are just a damn fool, John Henry Fox. Walk—*khong, khong, khong*[108]—run away now, Chaplain, because this isn't what you are here for, and it's just plain-ass nuts for us to even be even having this conversation. I'm nuts, and you're for damn sure nuts! *Niem vinh du duoc to chuc trong cai chet cua nhung nguoi van con song.*"[109]

---

106 "North Vietnam uniformed soldiers."
107 "Monkey"
108 "No, no, no"
109 "Honor within death is only celebrated by those that are still alive."

"All right, look, Gunny Mac, that was truly an impressive speech, but we have been through some pretty hairy things together. If there was absolutely no flipping chance of our ever coming back; well, I don't think that you are gungy enough to try this; right? I just never knew you to purposely buy into a one-way ticket home before. We were, and we still are, like brothers. Time, rank, or duties cannot replace that, nor will it ever be replaced unless it is you or me that wants that. Remember, you and I faced some pretty impossible times together, so if I don't go along with you who will have your six covered? That FNG spotter won't have it covered, because he will not be able to check his own weak-ass six. Let me say one thing here; you hard-headed Marine. You can take the chaplain out of the *Bac Si*,[110] but you can never … *ever* take the Doc out of the chaplain. I am your six, and that's that. I'm in on this mission, so shut up and brief me right after you pour each of us one more for luck."

"*O con lua dau toi*[111] Chaplain, Doc, or whoever the hell you are at this very moment, can you conjure up a couple of angels to go along with me or us? The Archangel Michael would even be better to tag along, because he would be able to take the heat off of me. Okay, Ensign Sir, my desperation conquers my common sense. I'll have a ghillie suit for you to wear, and I'll take care of your .45, KA-Bar and all of the other duce gear that you'll need.

"I am nuts for even thinking or doing this, Doc Fox, because we are going to be in some pretty heavy jungle, and I plan to leave the M-14 at home. It will just get us tangled up if we have to boogie, and, in all probability, we will have to run for our very lives.

"I'll take care of that numb-nutted PFC by telling him that I won out on not taking him along on the mission. Hopefully, we'll be back before anyone figures it out. I suppose if all goes well, there will be no court martial in this for me or for us. No one here really

---
110
111 "Oh, my aching ass."

knows you, and we'll paint up your ugly face with some extra camo makeup. So double-time and get the things you need, and then get back here ASAP. You're going to shit yer knickers when I tell you what we are actually going to be doing and where we are going to be doing it."

As the ensign was leaving, he turned back to me with more of his words of wisdom. "Gunny Mac, I think it best if you pass on referring to me as anything but *Bac Si* for the remainder of this mission. Neither of us will be wearing any rank insignia, and, in fact, I still have my old corpsman bag with me, so I'll just bring it along, just for some good Irish luck."

I just sat there, shaking my head. "Oh, Lord, I can't believe that we are going to do this, Fox, but I guess that we'll face the consequences if and when we get back. Hey Doc! Welcome aboard the insane train that'll be making stops in both heaven and hell!"

We sat up the remainder of the night as I laid out almost the entire complete mission for him. I drew the layout of the POW camp for him, but I left out one crucial part of the story—if I had to make the shot that I dreaded to even think about, Doc would not know about it until it was already a done deal. Moreover, if it did become necessary for me to take that shot, it would rest solely on me and no one else. If I should get taken out, Mister Fox could say, in all honesty, that he knew nothing of the second part of our mission.

So it is, and so it shall be, but I still wasn't feeling very damn gungy about this mission at the moment—but then again … I was a corporal once before and I guessed that I could be one again.

Now the time to talk had turned into a time to act.

*   *   *

Normally, we would have put on our hot and stinking ghillie when we got closer to our drop-off point. However, should we run into someone that knew that the numb-nutted PFC was six inches shorter and maybe sixty-five pounds lighter than John, it would be harder for them to spot.

We left for the helipad more than a half-hour before we were supposed to go, and we found that they were just fueling up the Huey when we got there. I told the warrant officer who was to fly us into our drop point that we truly needed more dark time on the ground, so if we could, we'd like to boogie ASAP. Thankfully, he nodded his head in agreement.

The flat-black, covert Huey lifted off the pad a good twenty-five minutes early, so we had covered our tracks thus far. Once we were in the air, we both removed the top of our ghillie suits for some cool, morning air, and so that we could breathe a bit. I thought about telling John all about Sarah, but there had not been time before the mission. It would have to wait for a better time and place than this. Besides I was supposed to get pictures from her on my next trip to Saigon and I was going to take a week off once this mission was over.

Talking in a Huey is damn near impossible if you don't have a headset on, which we didn't. Fox nudged me with his elbow to get my attention, and, when I looked over at him, he folded his palms together, gesturing to me that he was going to say a prayer. I just bowed my head and looked at him as his lips were moving, because I was sure he could pick a lot better words than I ever could have. Maybe because he would *ask* God to help us, and I would try to *tell* him to help us.

There were no lights on inside the chopper, so we already had our night-vision before we finally touched down. As we got in close to our drop point, they muffled down the chopper and came in fast and low. The skids weren't even on the dirt yet when the chopper began to pull back up and left us there, proned out in the inky black of the night.

Chapter 17

We hit the ground, our weapons at the ready to see if we were alone or not. We couldn't have put up much of a fight if they were to attack us anyway, because one bolt-action Remington and two .45s were no match for even one Kalashnikov AK-47 or SKS rifle.

We laid there a while in the tall grass, just listening to the sounds of the night and getting orientated. It is amazing when it is pitch dark just how many sounds there are. As close as we were together, I still had trouble seeing Doc lying right there next to me. How in the name of silence can some bugs and frogs make so damn much noise?

When I turned to him to nod that we were going to move out, he had a grin on his face like he was reliving the past. If it weren't for my standing orders that I might have to kill a US Naval Aviator, I guess I would have been grinning too, but I wasn't even cracking a smile under the circumstances.

Now we had a hard-ass two-plus-hour hump ahead of us, with absolutely no margin for resting or error. We stayed clear of the rutted and narrow road, because often there would probably be booby traps that were either in close or on the road itself. It wasn't the easiest way in for us, but for right now, it was our best choice as it was the only choice anyway.

The past four years of college life were starting to kick Doc's ass just a bit, but he kept right up with me and never made so much as one sorrowful groan. I thought what a spectacular team we still were—as improbable and as unlikely as a B-movie plot, but here we were, on our way to our objective at last.

Doc had taken out the map and compass, and he was pointing toward a small mountain that was off to our left. "That would be our objective right there, Gunny—hill 289. Let's get up there before the entire North Vietnam Army gets out of their nest, hive, or whatever it is that they sleep in."

That was the last time we spoke to each other, because everything from that point we either mimed or used hand signals. We were now in a time warp that had taken us back to more than four years ago and, for the moment, nothing much seemed to have changed.

Moving through the bush was a little tougher going, but if the paths had *punji* sticks,[112] booby traps, and trip wires, they would most assuredly ruin our early morning stroll. These people were absolute masters of inflicting pain and death with nature's bountiful bits and pieces at their disposal.

With all the vegetation we were encountering, I was worried that we might not find enough of a clearing to be able to see the tower; that was assuming that we even found the camp at all, of course. I'd had the opportunity to look at some recent air-recon photographs of the area yesterday, and they were a big help, because the maps we had sucked. I had one of the photo-interpreter guys do some updates on our one-to-fifty-thousand map, or we would have been lost for sure. I was able to snag three of the photos to make sure we were on target as we approached our objective hill overlooking the camp.

If we had to find this stinking place in the dark with only that

---

112 Sharpened bamboo sticks placed in a camouflaged hole, angled down to impale you as you instinctively pull your leg up to escape.

POS map, we would be damn lucky, and if we weren't, we'd all just be completely shit outta luck. People were gonna die.

As we got closer to our objective, we began to crawl along very slowly. *Creep* was actually a better word, as it becomes necessary to keep low, without making the bush or anything else move above or around you. Every time I did this, I'd think of Staff Sergeant O'Donnell standing in the range tower, watching over us. He was a tough taskmaster—as well, he should have been, because it was our own lives that depended on what he was teaching us. He had been here and done this so many times, I believe that he could crawl up to you and untie your boots without you knowing that he was even there.

He'd stand up there in that tower watching for us, and when he saw just one single person, he'd fire his M-16 in the air to let you know that you had all been burned, big time. When we were training, he was one tough-ass son of a bitch. He said he would not be responsible for any one of us getting killed or captured if we got in a hurry or got careless. After all of the mental abuse he could dish out to us, he'd still come and sit on a rack in our hooch and tell us about what we screwed up, and then what to do to fix it the next time. "It's your life," he'd say to us—and then, finally and ultimately, it was his own life that was gone.

One time I asked him about how many kills he had obtained as a sniper.

"Why do you ask me that?" he growled. "Just how is that important to you or to me at this point? We don't have a quota out in the bush, and we don't get a bonus just for doing our job. When you start to add up the numbers of kills you'd made, you'll eventually become a statistic—another number yourself. You just have to worry about one man, that one shot at one time. One shot and one kill is all you ever need to concentrate on; do you understand me?"

Yes, I did!

Waiting was always the worst part for me, because I am too

impatient, and I always want to charge forward, like George Custer. I kept reminding myself of the outcome of Custer and his command at the Little Big Horn, so I moved on, low and slow.

Okay, so go easy and go slow now, marine sniper, I thought. Move, stop, breathe, look and then listen. If you do this as he taught, you may live to see another day. One more time now: move, stop, breathe, look and then listen. Speed will get your ass compromised every single time. If you are out there watching and looking for them, they are out there watching and *looking for you in return.*

Staff Sergeant O'Donnell had a big sign behind his desk that has stayed with me even in my sleep. It read: "If you are not practicing, then someone, somewhere *is* practicing, and when you meet them ... you will die!"

The morning air was cool, but with this ghillie suit on, I felt like I was a Thanksgiving turkey still in the oven.

Doc touched the bottom of my boot. I looked back at him as he made a fist, shaking it a bit. He wanted a moment to get our bearings and to shoot an azimuth, so I just laid there while he fiddle-fucked around with his compass.

We only had about half an hour before first light came, and we needed to find a spot to hunker down pretty soon. I was glad John was there with me, though, because he handled a compass like his ass was actually magnetic north.

Doc touched my boot again and pointed off to his right. He held up four fingers and then a closed fist, indicating that we would move in that direction about forty meters.

We were approaching a slight rise, so I stopped and held my flat hand up, indicating that he should stop where he was. I moved on ahead, craning my neck to try and see over the rise. If he was right on the money, I should be able to peer down into the valley to where the POW camp was supposed to be located. At this point, it was still too dark to see far enough or to make anything out.

Doc crept up beside me and started to set up his spotting scope. Each move he made was very slow, very deliberate, and very calculated. The moves were almost exaggerated to prevent any telltale sound or click that could possibly give us away.

God, I was hoping that, when some light allowed us to see enough of the valley, the camp would be right there below us, where we were supposed to be.

The SEALs and our own Marine Force Recon people should have made their way to their intended position already. So many pieces of the puzzle still had to come together that it was still impossible for me to see the entire picture at this point.

As we lay there, waiting for first light, I wanted very badly to ask the padre to say a prayer. I wanted reaffirmation that we were in the right place at the right time, and that we could make our kill shots.

I wondered if that was really a legitimate request for me to pray about, because I guess that I had always just assumed that God was on our side of this stinking-ass war. Maybe God doesn't choose sides in a war. Maybe He just sits back and shakes His head as He watches on. This would be a good question for me to ask the chaplain about—if or when we got back home.

The morning sun began to creep up and over the mountain, slowly spilling down into the valley below us. As we lay there, I saw the dip where the camp should be, but it was now temporarily shrouded in a foggy mist. It would take a while longer for the fog to burn off, but that wouldn't keep the NVA from rolling out of the sack and making ready for the day. I hate to wait like this ... damn it, damn it, damn it!

I wondered what if this were the day they were going to hit the Ho Chi Minh Trail with the POWs in tow. I imagined if that were to take place, they would run right into the Force Recon and SEAL team assembled a short distance from the gate. I needed to quit conjuring up hypothetical situations and focus on what was in front of me. Like Jack Webb said on *Dragnet*: "The facts ma'am, just the facts."

I slowly reached under the neck of my ghillie and pulled out a small, white piece of cloth from Sarah's *ao dai*. The sweetness of her smell was long gone from the soft silk, but a vision of her lingered on with me for just a moment. I could almost see and feel her lying there in our bed, sleeping so peacefully. Lord, what I would give to be there, next to my wife, and not out here in the miserable, stinking jungle, ready and waiting to kill other people.

It was 0646 when the fog began to lift enough to make out an image of the camp and the tower below us. This veiled image of it all told me that we were at least in the correct spot. A huge part of the puzzle just fell into place for us at this minute. Doc and I now had piqued our interest as we began to study each detail as it began to show itself. John tapped my arm and pointed toward the tower. He studied once again, this time under eight-power from his scope. He then held up one finger and pointed back at it.

I looked through my rifle scope again to confirm what I thought I had already seen. There were not two sentries in the tower like there were supposed to be—instead only one was visible. Maybe I just had one shot to make this morning. I nodded my head as I snuggled the butt of my rifle up and into my right shoulder. I took a deep breath and started to release it. The man in the tower was looking around with his binoculars, but not showing any real interest as he scanned right on past where we were.

Now take one more deep breath, I thought, and let it out slowly. I began to squeeeeze the trigger and take up the trigger slack to make that perfect headshot. The crosshairs from the scope were now perched perfectly on his nose.

Wait, wait, *wait*, I thought. Something was wrong; something was very wrong here. Goddamn it what the fuck was going on down there? Was that bastard chewing his breakfast, or is he talking to someone? I took my eye away from the scope and lowered the butt of my rifle. John now looked at me with a quizzical expression on his face as I held up one finger, shook my head no and I held up a second finger, pointing back toward the tower. I believed that the second enemy sentry was lying there on the floor, and that the two of them were actually talking to each other. Fox looked through his scope for about thirty seconds before nodding his head *yes* to me. Now he could see the other man starting to move around also.

Doc rechecked the windage for me and gave me my thumbs up, indicating that nothing had changed from the dope he had previously given to me. I could take my shot when I was ready.

Okay, once again, take a deep breath and then release it, I thought as I began taking up the tension on the trigger. Slow, slow, very slow … as the second breath left my lungs, the rifle jumped inexpediently and kicked my shoulder. I watched the soldier drop his now-shattered binoculars and grab the remnants of his face as his head snapped back from the impact of the bullet. Oh, that was just absolutely beautiful—a near-perfect headshot. I worked the bolt back, ejecting the empty brass and jamming it forward once again as I chambered a new 7.62 caliber match round.

I was just releasing my breath once again as the second enemy solder popped up. He was already grabbing for the Soviet-made Kord 12.7-millimeter heavy machine gun as he looked up the hill toward us. He paused for just a half-second as he tried to see where we were, but he didn't have to look very long. The bullet impacted his sternum and ripped through his chest, heart, and spine, knocking him backward far enough that he fell out of the tower. That just brought the promising army career for two enemy soldiers to a screeching halt! *Xin loi*, ya all!

I quickly recovered and chambered a third round to cover the Special Ops guys that should just now be charging the bamboo gate of the POW camp. I was truly hoping they would be able to recover and remove the three Americans so another round would not become necessary. This was the shot I was dreading to make. I wondered what the chaplain lying next to me would think if I had to shoot this US Navy lieutenant commander. Lord knows that would change the entire completion of the mission for both of us.

Chapter 18

As I was absorbed in watching our guys through the riflescope, my rifle absolutely *exploded* from my grasp! It kicked me on the right side of my head like a football punter had just used my skull as his ball.

I was seriously dazed, but the pain came through loud and clear—instantly and without remorse!

I never did hear the crack of the rifle that had nearly severed my head from my shoulders. The Chinese-made bullet had struck the Redfield scope, shattering it in half and leaving two worthless pieces that were no longer attached to each other. The bullet had also creased my left cheek, finally burying itself just above the armpit. I tried to move my arm, but apparently the round had broken my shoulder, because any further attempt caused me excruciating pain. I was trying desperately to not scream, but mostly what I absolutely had to do was to remain conscious.

I guess what I'd heard was true, though—you never hear the one shot that eventually gets you.

I rolled onto my left side from the impact of the bullet as I was trying desperately to recover and get back to my rifle, but my shoulder wasn't cooperating.

I was still trying to figure out what the hell had just taken place and where that round had come from. A half-second later, a second bullet impacted the tree that was right next to me, just about an inch away from my head. I damn well heard *that* shot!

Damn it all to hell! Now I knew that there was an enemy sniper out there, and he was dead-ass sighted in on me.

I suppose it was pure instinct for me to raise my head once more to peer around for him, but then a third round slammed into the dirt directly in front of my nose. I quickly reassessed that decision. Although he hit me once and missed me twice, I knew that the next round was probably going to be my one-way ticket home. This sucker was a damn good shot!

From to my right side, I could see Doc as he hastily came rolling toward me. Shit; I wondered if maybe he had been hit too. In a moment like this one, time and space compress so fast that your brain is still trying to assemble the impossible and then make it at least probable.

John looked over at me and at my bleeding shoulder for a second before he nodded his head. I wasn't sure of what in the hell he was nodding his head about, but if I would have had more time to think about it, I think I would have been pissed!

When the sniper shot me, Doc had quickly swung his scope in the direction of the shot and saw a possible image and smoke from the shooter up in a tree.

He took my trashed rifle and began pounding the broken scope off of it with his own scope. The glass and fragments of both of them flew all over me as he ejected the already chambered round and chambered another one. From his vantage point, he had a tiny bit of brush between him and the NVA sniper, so that may have made him invisible from the enemy's view.

I calmly said, "Can you see him, John?"

There was no answer from him. "*Doc!*" I now shouted. "Do you know where the …?"

The rifle bolted upward as it discharged, splattering my face with unburned powder and a blast that went way beyond any conceivable level of pain to my ears. The muzzle of the Remington was less than a foot from my head when he'd fired, and the pain from it was nearly as bad as my shoulder wound. My ear was screaming, but the screeching sounded like my head was inside a fifty-five gallon oil drum with a freight train roaring over me.

What in the hell was he doing, bluffing the enemy sniper or what? Doc quickly followed with one more shot, thus emptying the weapon. He grabbed up another five round box of match grade ammo and quickly fired them, one right after the other.

"I think I got 'im," he said.

"*What?*" I yelled back to him. His lips moved, but I was beyond hearing anything more than the thunderous ringing and throbbing in my right ear.

He turned to me and leaned in closer. "I think I got him, Gunny. I'm sure he fell about fifteen feet out of a tree; that is, about four hundred meters from us."

He babbled something else to me as he ripped open a large bandage, and poured something on it, and smashed it onto my open wound. He then dropped a triangular bandage next to the Remington. What was I supposed to do with this? A bird can't fly with one wing, and I can't put that on with one hand. Fuck me hard!

Okay, thanks, Doc. That hurt like a real son-of-a-bitch! Just one more time through the frigg'n hurt locker, and I figured I'd pass out.

I wanted to say there was no fucking way that Doc just made a four-hundred-meter shot with open sights, but unless that asshole jumped out of that tree, maybe he did.

Before I could say anything else, he jumped up and went running down the hill with his .45 waving around his head like he was John fucking Wayne. Heroes are generally just a split-second between a stupid decision and a lot of damn good luck. I hoped that luck was running alongside that US Navy chaplain right now, because he'd just left common sense behind.

Why was he going down there all alone? I couldn't rise up to see where he went, so I just laid back and applied some more pressure onto my bleeding shoulder. The pain was now becoming unbearable, and I struggled to remain conscious. My immediate thoughts were of my wife, Sarah. Shit, it just came to me that I didn't have time my insurance changed, and I was still working on the immigration papers for the embassy. I can't die; I gotta fight for her—for us!

"Don't you fucking die you stupid bastard" I muttered to no one.

My head was spinning at a high rate of inconclusive thought. With the shoulder wound, the shock of being shot, and the proximity of my head to the muzzle of the rifle, I was definitely out of the fight for a while.

My hearing was trying to return, and I make out some sounds through the painful, hollow-sounding ringing in my ears. I was pretty sure they were shots coming up from the valley below me, but that was still only a possibility. I wasn't sure if it was the SEALs wiping up their part of the mission, or if it was that whacko corpsman-slash-chaplain putting that frick'n sniper down for the count. Maybe it was the sniper taking John out; maybe the SEALs never made it to the gate. Maybe if pigs had wings they could fly …What the fuck?

Now it became clear to me why that sniper was out there. With the tower guards gone, there was only one way for our guys to approach the camp. He could have picked off each and every one of them from his location. I had foiled that for him, so he had to get me first, because I would have nailed him with the third round that I had already chambered.

I just hoped that the three pilots were freed, or this mission just pissed backward for nothing! Fuck me hard, I thought, can anything else possibly go wrong?

That bastard had broadsided me, because I never thought there was anyone else out there. I got careless, and I should have remembered what Staff Sergeant O'Donnell told us about not being alone in the hunt. "If you are out there hunting them, they are out there hunting you!" Too late for thinking about that for now, I guess. Sorry, Staff Sergeant O'Donnell, I fucked up royally.

If the sniper had been watching me for very long, he would have capped me right off, so I guess he didn't know we were there until I had already eliminated the two soldiers in the tower. I figured that he must have been up in the tree all night, because he damn sure didn't climb up that tree after morning light had come.

Damn, damn, *dammit*! How in the hell did I let all of this slide right on past me! Son of a bitch—I can't even think straight now.

"Fuck me hard," I muttered.

This guy just had to be one of the top NVA snipers, because the shot he made was one hell of a lot harder to pull off than mine was. Damn my arrogance, and damn my lack of attention to detail. I'd bet that the Komodo Dragon didn't screw up like I'd just done!

I laid there, still straining to hear, and I was trying to think about how much time we had to make it out to our pick-up point. It occurred to me that the last shooting I thought I heard down in the valley may well have been the enemy sniper killing John. Just because the enemy fell out of the tree didn't mean he was dead, and Doc couldn't be so sure that is what he actually saw from this distance. Damn it, I couldn't even think straight anymore.

One thing was for damn sure, and that was that this entire area would soon be crawling with enemy zipper-heads. I didn't have any hope of our making the pick-up point on my own and in the condition I was experiencing. For that matter, I might not make it even if Fox did return pretty soon.

I guess my arrogant immunity to war and wounds had just come face to face with reality as the immensity of this whole shitty mess began to set in. I took my .45 from the holster and cocked the hammer back. The prospect of saving the last bullet for myself had just become a reality and not just some bravado leatherneck boast made at the club after consuming a pitcher or two of beer. Now the bullshit caught up with as I reminded myself to count how many rounds I'd shot so that I'd keep one. I even considered whether I should put the barrel to my temple or under my chin.

Doc and the captured prisoner were already on top of me when I could finally hear them coming up the hill. The sniper was being herded along by John, with a .45 pointed squarely at his back. When they arrived, Doc pushed the enemy soldier down to his knees. He quickly bound his mouth and his wrists. It was a good thing that Doc had brought along his old medical pack, as he now used the tape from his kit to secure the new POW.

I was attempting to get up when Doc grabbed the top of my ghillie suit and pulled me up and onto my feet. "Are you okay to travel now, Gunny? We gotta *di-di mau.*"

Doc was hastily tying the triangular bandage into a sling for my left shoulder. As he finished, he handed me a morphine syrette, which I immediately stuck into my leg.

Ahhhhh, some relief at last, woohoo!

I was pissed, and I snapped at John, "I would like to have had just a moment to interrogate this enemy bastard before you taped up his mouth up, Doc."

"Listen to me, Gunny. If you want to take time to BS with this sniper as to why he shot at you or why two other rounds missed, we might be the ones getting interrogated. I really think it is prudent for us to go far, far away from here first, and then you can shoot the shit with this enemy sniper later."

I could see some blood staining the enemy's right abdomen, and it looked like he had sustained a through-and-through shot that might have missed his vital organs. The fall out of the tree probably hurt him more than the gunshot. One thing was for damn sure, and that was this guy was in a lot better shape than I was.

"All right, let's head 'em up and move 'em out … assholes and elbows," I almost yelled as Doc picked up the Remington rifle and holstered his .45 auto.

I couldn't resist getting at least one thought into his gook's head should I die in the next few minutes: "*Ngay cuab ban la hoan tat ban khi duoi xe, nhung thoi diem thuc te khi ket thuc den voi toi bay gio ban fucking can ba ban tia.*"[113]

John pushed the prisoner off in a direction that would hopefully take us back toward our pick-up point in the least amount of time. This was not quite the way we planned our exit, but it was the most expeditious and, unfortunately, the most reckless way back to the road. Time was not on our, side and we couldn't afford to waste precious minutes at this juncture.

Most of our movement was downhill, but the enemy kept falling down from the deep jungle brush that kept tripping him up. It was hard enough for the two of us to run without our hands bound up behind us, so this guy was doing some serious double gainers as he'd crash and burn. Doc would immediately snatch him back upright and then push him off once again. At one point, he went crashing headfirst, right into the ground and rolling into a tree. At that point, he lost the American-made Boonie-cover he was wearing. I momentarily marveled at an enemy soldier having that long of hair way out here in the bush. Almost all of them I ever saw shaved their heads like we did, simply to prevent bugs from taking up residence on our gourds.

---

[113] "Your day is finished, you monkey's ass, but the actual moment it finishes is now up to me, you fucking sniper scum!"

I wondered why Doc looked over at me and motioned toward the sniper while he was showing me a big grin on his face. This seemed a bit out of character for him because he was generally the more serious one between the two of us.

We were trying hard to keep some semblance of quiet while we were crashing through the bush, but, right now, speed was a higher priority than stealth. We were supposed to be at our pick-up point right fucking now, and we still a long way. Bend me over again— we've already lost our ride home and that was for damn sure.

Fox was just in front of me and the prisoner when we all came roaring into a small clearing that had been an enemy camp at some time. Directly in front of us were three Viet Cong soldiers sitting near a field radio and cooking their rice. I didn't know who was more surprised to see whom, but we were all caught off guard by coming face to face like that.

Doc was carrying the Remington rifle at the grip rather than slung on his shoulder, so he just pointed and fired it from his hip. It was a great shot, considering the speed he had to make it. The Remington is a bolt-action rifle, so he only had that one round available without jacking another into the chamber. It took that first VC right back off of his feet as he was standing up to grab for his rifle, though.

That gave us the crucial element of surprise while we were hauling ass right on through the clearing. As we boogied on past them, I was able to fire off a full magazine of seven .45 rounds, thus taking out the other two bad guys as they tried to reach for their rifles. It was their bad idea for having stacked their weapons today, but we needed every huss that came our way right now.

There were actually three things working in our behalf: one, they were caught completely off guard by us; two was the element of surprise that always works well for you in warfare; the third one was that they were just plain old careless and apparently ill-trained

VC. The old Marine Corps saying was so true: when the fit hits the shan, you'll fight as you train, and train as you'll fight.

If they would have been regular *Bo Doi* sitting there instead of these Viet Cong, we would have been toast, and our prisoner would ultimately end holding the winning poker hand.

That whole incident started and finished in a matter of seconds, but it proved to us that, while we were deep in enemy territory, these dumb clucks felt too much false security. "*Xin Loi, khong co noi nguoi chien thang thu hai trong mot sung chien dau.*"[114]

---

[114] "Sorry about that, there is no second-place winner in a gunfight."

Chapter 19

We got to a small rut of a road and stopped to grab our breath. The enemy sniper had taken a beating, falling so many times with his hands tied behind his back, but I still had absolutely no remorse nor sympathy for him. Fortunately for me, the morphine was keeping me going.

John reached over to the prisoner, pulling up the long, black, loose hair as if he were showing off a trophy to me. "Have you figured this whole thing out yet, Gunny Mac?"

"Figured what out?" I said, still not grasping the obvious. "Doc, can you put another patch over this for me, I need to try and stop the bleeding, or I'll run out of my red juices pretty soon. I'll say one thing about this damn sniper—he's exceptionally good at what he does."

"You still haven't figured it out yet have you, Gunny? You really don't get it, do you?"

Okay, I was missing something that mister butthead thought was important. "Hey what the fuck, Doc? Are we going to play *What's My Line* right here and now? You must think you are Charles Daly hosting *What's My Line* on TV?"

By this time Fox was laughing so hard he had tears rolling down his cheeks. "Your sniper has breasts, Gunny. He's a she."

I just stood there, dumbfounded, trying to make all of this fit somehow. A sniper with tits?

"The Dragon?" I hissed. I frantically looked at John and repeated, "Oh, my God, Doc … he … she has to be the Komodo Dragon then!" John still had a blank look on his face. "It's gotta be her, Doc, it just has to be her!" Of course, John didn't know about this dragon woman, nor her reputation as a killing machine. He did not have the hatred for her that I had already developed.

I snarled *"Di mi ami di"*[115] I glared at her as all the air inside me exhausted from my body. "You motherfucking ruthless son of a bitch! *Ban key get nguoi ac dam.*[116] Get away from her, Fox. Move away, 'cause I am going to put a bullet right between her gook running lights!"

I pulled my .45 out of the holster, dropped the empty magazine out of it, and reloaded a full one as she stared at me with utter contempt and total silence. As I pointed it at her head, I quipped, *"Ban dung dang chet bay gio. Toi se get ban."*[117]

Doc was obviously agitated, because time was definitely not on our side. *"Stop it, Gunny*, we don't have time for this bullshit. She is a prisoner of war, and you aren't going to shoot her with her hands taped behind her back."

I smirked and said, "Sure I can, and that's far less than what she deserves. You have no idea with whom we are dealing here, Doc. This bitch is the Komodo Dragon, and you are pissing on the graves of twenty marines by protecting her. You can pray for all of them later, but this pond scum will die for what she has done. Move the fuck away from her!"

"Gunny, you can't be sure this is the sniper called the Komodo Dragon. The NVA has dozens of women snipers, so we'll take her in

---

[115] "You motherfucking bitch!"
[116] "You sadistic killer."
[117] "You deserve to die and I am going to kill you."

as a POW. Come on, Gunny, you are a better marine than this, and you know that we are a member of the Geneva Convention."

Fuck the goddamned Geneva Convention! We belong, and they don't, so there are no stupid-ass rules to war or dying.

We were at a standoff, and there was nothing else that would give back the honor to the marines that she had tortured so ruthlessly and then killed.

I was 100 percent sure of who this woman was, and there could only be the one and only Komodo. I didn't care if I stood right here and bled to death, because she was going to die—she had to die because I had vowed to get, and now I had her there, right in front of me.

I growled, *"Chien tranh khong phai la mot loi xin loi de tan va giet chet nhumg cho tat ca ban da lam tru oc day ban se bay gio tieu thu tinh vinh hang trong dia nguc. Toi the nguyen de ket thuc day curong cua cac ban cua su dau va torture va vi the giup do toi chua troi. Toi se song de chi nhin thay ban chet!"*[118]

Our brief argument was shattered by the sound of a vehicle coming toward us on the piece-of-shit road. It should have been one of theirs, because we were still deep into Indian country, but it had the unmistakable sound of an American jeep.

John and I both looked at each other with the same question. We didn't speak; we flung our bodies off the road and into the brush for some semblance of concealment.

Shit that hurt my shoulder, and it just started bleeding even more after that outstanding stunt. When Doc flew off of the road, he had a very firm grip on Komodo, because if she would have gone into the bush with me, my KA-Bar would have silenced her forever. I could actually taste the contentment of slicing her neck open from

---

[118] "War isn't an excuse to torture and kill, but for all you have done in your past you will now spend eternity in hell. I vowed to end your reign of pain and torture, and so help me God, I am going to live just to see you die."

her trachea all the way to the evil spine that held her slimy-ass head on her shoulders. The funny thing was that I felt so much love for one Vietnamese woman and an equal amount of hate for another. Love and war make such a piss-poor combination of emotions!

The jeep bounced along the road slowly, because this road was actually used more for the foot porters than for vehicles. They carried rice, medicine, ammunition and the likes all the way from Hanoi or Haiphong, on their back to their final destination.

Very seldom was an NVA vehicle found in an open area during daylight hours. They would slither out from under their camouflage netting when it was dark, unless they had the cover of triple-canopy jungle to hide under.

As clever as they thought they were, we were flying missions more at night and utilizing infrared imaging or SLAR.[119] An IR image or return could determine what kind of vehicle this hot spot came from if it was in the hands of a good photo imagery interpreter at CICV.

I chanced a quick glance as the jeep was passing me. It was an American AN/MRC-87 radio jeep being driven by what appeared to be a marine. This dumb shit could have only gotten lost at the fork in the road several miles back. A couple more miles driving in the direction, he was headed he too would be either a POW or KIA.

Worse yet, the NVA would get their slimy dick-skinner hands on a sophisticated, state-of-the-art radio that was capable of transmitting any place in the world. No doubt there was one or more crypto-authentication book on board too. It was time to end this asshole's Sunday drive before he provided Hanoi and the Soviet Union a precious gift from the United States.

I got to my feet with considerable pain and effort and stepped onto the badly rutted road.

119 Side-looking airborne radar

"Hey, you stupid ass bastard, where in the fuck are you going?" I was shouting as I struggled to catch up with the vehicle. This wasn't a swift tactical move on my part, but I was already pretty sure that the bad guys already knew about where we were.

The jeep lurched to a stop alongside of Doc and Komodo, with John already pointing the rifle at the numb-nutted marine that was driving.

The kid was actually attempting to pull his .45 pistol from the holster. I bellowed "No, no, no; don't you even think of doing that, you dumb-ass!"

I walked over to the driver's side of the jeep casually holding my right hand out to him. "Give me the weapon, marine," I said. This kid was so scared that he was already shaking like a dog shitting peach seeds.

"Are you American?" he asked.

I was flabbergasted. "No, shithead," I growled back at him, "I am your fucking Uncle Ho Chi Minh! Who in the hell do you think I am, and what in God's name are you doing here? You must be deserting to other side to sell them this radio jeep."

"Hell no, sir! This radio crapped out, so I'm taking it back to the place that is marked on this map. I musta missed a turn or something like that, sir."

"Quit calling me sir," I instinctively replied. "He is a sir, and I'm a gunny."

John lowered the rifle, but he obviously wasn't impressed nor was he smiling.

"Does this radio work at all?" I asked the visibly shaken marine.

"I think it does sometimes, but then again maybe it won't. There must be a loose connection someplace, sir." the kid stammered.

I climbed into the backseat as best I could. "Get this jeep turned around, shithead, because grab-ass time is over for all of us."

I glanced toward John and Komodo, telling him to keep her ass covered with something that could kill her if she decided to break dirty on him.

"Let's see if this is still our lucky day," I muttered as I powered up the radio and dialed in the confidential frequency that I needed to communicate with a confidential someone that was somewhere … confidential of course.

"Blue Boy, Blue Boy, this is Chime Whiskey, over."

There was nothing but squelch responding to my call, but the radio looked as if it was transmitting. "Come on, you lousy bastards, talk to me," I mumbled to myself.

One more time, I thought. "Blue Boy, Blue Boy, this is Chime Whiskey, *over!*" If I would have had enough smarts to be scared, this would have been an ideal time.

Then there came an answer to my call. "Chime Whiskey, this is Blue Boy on priority-one traffic net, please authenticate Tango, Uniform, Papa for me, Chime Whiskey."

"Oh, my aching grunt ass!" I hissed at the uncaring radio. "Look, Blue Boy, I am Ghost Rider, so you look that info up pronto, because I don't have any authentication, nor do I have any time to play your stupid-ass games. Understand that this is *flash* traffic, Blue Boy, I repeat, *flash* traffic … Do you copy me? *Over!*"

"Okay, Ghost Rider, this is Blue Boy Six Actual, and the net is all yours, so send your traffic, over," a new and calm voice said. This was Six Actual, or the officer who the call sign was assigned to. Generally, I try to avoid talking to officers, but today was certainly going to be an exception.

I waved Doc over to me, and I asked him to give me the coordinates of our present location.

He pointed to a place on the map, "We are here, Gunny."

"Blue Boy, I need dust off[120] to respond to Lima Papa 453, Nora

---

120 Medical evacuation helicopters

Edward 413 on map number 416 for one WIA. This is priority one, do you copy, Blue Boy? Over."

Blue Boy confirmed the coordinates back to me and told me to wait and see if there was a dust off or any other kind of chopper in the vicinity.

A very long minute passed and Blue Boy came back on the air. "Okay, Ghost Rider, I've diverted Dust Off 121 to your location. They advise that they are already full up, but they can squeeze in one more, I repeat, one more only. Do you have yellow smoke, Ghost Rider? Over."

"Yellow smoke?" I grumbled to myself. "Negatory, that is a negative for any color of smoke. Advise dust off that I will use a signal mirror when they become visual. Also be advised that the LZ should now be considered as hostile; I say again, extremely hostile! Do you copy me on that? Over."

"That's affirm, sir. The ETA for Dust Off 121 to the LZ is expected to be zero five mikes[121] or less. Dust Off 121 also advises for you to be ready to go immediately because of their critical fuel restrictions. They can touch and go one time, but they cannot come around for you again Ghost Rider. Copy, copy? Over."

"That's affirm, Blue Boy, I copy you. Ghost Rider is closing the net at this time; roger and out."

I advised Doc that my ride was only about five minutes out, and they would have zero spare time within the hot LZ. I wanted to take Komodo along with me, but that was impossible for me to do, given the situation.

I dismounted the radio jeep and told the PFC to get his ass in gear and get the fuck out of Indian country. "Post haste, or we'll all become POWs; resulting from this clusterfuck. One of two things,

---

[121] Minutes

Doc. Either you kill that *gai diem*[122] or bring her slimy Asian ass back with you for the intel guys. Do read me, five-by-five, on that?"

Doc started to answer me, just as a sixty-millimeter mortar blew up fell about eighty meters short of us. That was followed by two more as the gooners began walking the HE [123]rounds in toward us.

At the same time, we also began to get hostile rifle fire from up on the side of the hill to our right. It was sporadic at first, but it was increasing rapidly and compromising the touch and go of my dust-off chopper.

"I think we have just been told in a very unprofessional and untimely manner to leave here, Doc." I was shedding off any excess equipment to reduce my air weight. "I'll move away from the road for my chopper ride, and I'll see you back at the OK Corral."

I saluted the ensign before I turned and double-timed away the best I could. Right now, I was running on pure adrenalin and morphine. A grin stretched across my face as I realized that was the first time that I'd ever saluted Ensign Fox. Maybe I was hoping that it wouldn't be the last time.

The army chopper was already thumping its way up the valley. I didn't have to signal the pilots flying the First Air Cavalry Huey, because they had already put an eyeball on me shuffling toward the LZ.

The Huey was coming in low and hot[124] as they bounced the skids on the dirt just one time. The soldier in the door was already grasping my right hand and pulling me up and into the chopper as it rebounded back up into the air.

The badly overloaded bird was seriously resisting gaining altitude with the extra weight of wounded on board. Each and every one of us was actually willing that son of a bitch up and as far away as it

---

122 "Whore."
123 High explosive
124 Fast

could take us. There wasn't time for praying, so that was the best thing available at the moment.

First there was the pure pucker factor that was immediate, and then came the willing, and that was usually followed by conscious prayer. Even to an atheist.

The mortar and rifle rounds were seriously closing in on us as the pilot did some pretty amazing maneuvers to avoid the ground fire. The skids were ripping the tops off of the trees while we were trying to make a slow climb out of the valley. We were such an easy target for every enemy weapon out there, but, for whatever reason, we skated clean. Call it luck or call it fate, but we managed it anyway.

I turned back around and I saw that the radio jeep was now making record time back toward the main road. I thought the reverend must have a pretty special relationship established with that big general up in the sky, because that stupid radio jeep sure as hell appeared out of nowhere like it did.

Lost, my ass! That PFC was either one lucky-ass jarhead, or he was hiding a huge pair of wings under his utility jacket—add a golden halo shining under his M-2 helmet also.

Come to think of it, how could he possibly make a wrong turn from a main road onto some POS, rutted path? Maybe this was divine intervention, who knows—but he certainly saved our bacon back there.

Chapter 20

The Huey landed on the hospital's emergency hot pad a short time later. I knew that I'd lost a considerable amount of blood, but I wasn't nearly as hammered as some of the others on board. There was blood all over the inside and on the deck of the Huey, and it stunk from burnt flesh. The blood on the deck of the chopper was already getting tacky, and it made a sickening, glue-like sucking sound with my every move. Those who could were attending to others while a medic grabbed my hand for me to hold a tourniquet in place on another soldier whose leg had been blown completely off. The outside air that was sweeping through the aircraft couldn't remove the stench of blood, puke, and burned flesh as the turbine engine began shrieking and smoking from the overload.

I know in my military mind that I owed my entire existence to all of the wounded men and her crew of four who diverted to pull me out of the bush.

There is no question that I would have never made it back to any place for medical attention without Dust Off 121 landing in the midst of mortar rounds dropping from the sky. I wish I could buy all of them a beer—or ten! These guys weren't about being heroes, however; for them, today was just another day at work, helping their brothers get a second chance at life.

As the other guys were quickly being offloaded from the chopper, I slid toward the door and placed my feet on the skid. I thought that I could make my own way to the row of ambulances that was standing by. Apparently, I was wrong.

The next thing I remembered was a navy nurse telling me that I was going into surgery to try and fix some severely torn tissue in my shoulder. Now there was the face and the voice of an absolute angel, even through my blurred vision from the meds I'd been given.

As I was falling asleep, I could both feel and smell my beautiful wife, Sarah, leaning over me. My head was resting against her breast, and my blue eyes were looking deep into her beautiful black, almond eyes. *Anh yeu em hai quan my toi. Ngu bay gio duct re toi nhu cau va chung toi se som nhat cung lam nua. Ban la tinh yeu toi va chung toi se nhanh chong chia ae dva tre chung ta tinh yeu chung tao. Trong khi chung toi bay gio la mot gia dinh.*"[125]

I could almost feel her beautiful long black hair when it was touched me as she leaned over me. It was hard for me to see her face, because there was an extremely bright, white light shining from right behind her head, and she truly looked like an angel to me.

* * *

Now comes the part of the story that I wouldn't be privy to for years to come. This information would have saved me a lot of grief, but regs are regs in our security world of need to know. I can tell this story—the complete story—now that I know everything.

The radio jeep was nearly impossible to keep seated in as the

---

[125] "I love you my American marine. Sleep now, my childlike boy, and we will soon be together once again. You are my love and we will soon also share our child of this love. We are now one family, forever."

PFC pushed it far beyond the conditions of the road. When they made it back to the fork, John told the driver to pull over and stop.

"I'll just be a couple minutes here as I take care of some critical business. You'd best just stay put here in the jeep," John ordered.

"Yes, Sir. Excuse me, sir, are you a sir?"

Fox just pointed to the seat and commanded, "Stay!"

He then took the woman from the backseat of the jeep, shoving her toward the bushes next to the road. John had his pistol pointed squarely at the back of her head as they trotted along.

Once they were out of sight, John told her, "*Dung lai!*"[126] The woman stopped, but she made no effort to turn around and face him. She would rather die with a bullet in the back of her head as a proud soldier that had been captured only by luck and fate. She knew that she'd fought well, and that she would not allow the American marine behind her to see the tears that were now welling up in her eyes. These were not tears of defeat or fear—she was proud, and she would die that exact same way. John silently cut the tape from her hands and slowly began pulling it away from her mouth. She turned to face him, her eyes ablaze with anger and contempt. However, she saw that his pistol was now holstered, and he indicated for her to lift her camouflage shirt where she had been shot.

"Do you know that I'm not the Komodo Dragon woman that your Gunny thinks I am?" she said, in near perfect English. "The Komodo Dragon is much younger than I am, but you can kill me now or as you wish, American marine sniper," she snapped.

John was shocked to hear the woman speaking English with a slight French accent.

"I don't know if you are the Komodo or not, but the Gunny sure is convinced that you are. I am going to treat your wound, and then

---

126 "Stop!"

I am going to release you, but it must appear to that other marine back in the jeep that I shot and killed you."

Her eyes softened, and she spoke with a questioning tone in her voice. "Why then will you release me, marine? I am the enemy solder that would have killed you and the other marine, like I should have. That was my intention, and I tried my very best to kill you."

"Yes, you are in fact the enemy, but you are not *my* enemy. Furthermore, I am not a marine. I'm in the US. Navy—a chaplain from Da Nang. Do you understand what a chaplain is?"

"Of course I do, but then why are you with a *nguoi ban tia*[127] that kills then?"

John told her that was a long story and there was no time for details. He quickly finished disinfecting the gunshot wound, which was a clean through-and-through, and then he gave her a morphine injection to take along with her. Obviously, there were no vital organs hit, or she would be dead or dying as they spoke.

"If you are not the Komodo Dragon, then who are you?" John continued working on her as they spoke.

"I am known as Ho Phi Nu, or Tiger Woman; and your name is—what? Please tell me, Chaplain."

"Fox; Ensign John Fox. Now you go, Ho Phi Nu, because we have taken way too much time already. Now! *Di-di!*"

"Father, I ask you to bless me please," Tiger Woman said as she knelt very slowly and gingerly.

John smiled. "Ho Phi Nu, I am not Catholic. I am Baptist minister. We pray, but we don't do blessings. God is with us both right now, and he will choose what is right, but you have to go right now." With that said, John helped her to stand up once again.

As she hesitantly turned away from him, he fired three bullets

127 "Sniper"

into the ground. He then turned away from her and double-timed back to the jeep without looking back toward the woman.

"Drive like the devil was behind you, Private, because I think he may very well be. Let's get out of here while we still can."

The PFC did as he was told, but looked over at John and asked, "Jeez, sir. Did you really just kill her? I mean, you really just shot that woman and left her for dead back there?"

"Let me explain something to you, marine. You accidently got involved in a classified mission. What you saw and all of the people you saw here today never existed. You got lost, and then you found your way back without incident and on your own. Is that clear?"

"Well, I guess so, sir ..."

"Don't you try to guess anything, PFC, just listen up! You are aware of Portsmouth Naval Prison, I assume? If you want to remain a PFC or ever see lance corporal, then you got lost, and you never saw anything. Is that infinitely clear to you?"

"Yes, sir. It is perfectly clear. I never saw anything, I just got lost, like you said, sir! Lost, I just got myself lost, I think." For the remainder of the drive, the private never looked side to side; his eyes remained drilled on the road.

When the jeep got close to the gate, Doc told him to pull over and stop. As John got out, he thanked the PFC for the ride.

"You're welcome, sir, but if I never saw you before, how can you be thanking me right now?"

"I think there is hope for you to make lance corporal someday now, son. Bless you and have a safe tour in Vietnam," John said as he patted the young marine on his shoulder.

*   *   *

When I finally began to come around after an intense four-hour surgery, Fox was sitting in a hospital chair, sleeping. I mumbled something, and John opened his eyes and begrudgingly sat up.

He smiled. "They were out of your blood type, Gunny, so they gave you tiger piss instead of blood. How are you feeling?"

"I'm feeling like I just got shot, Chaplain. Pray tell, how in the hell do you think I should be feeling at this very moment?"

John said, "The doctor told me that you need some pretty intense reconstructive surgery, and that you will be sent to Balboa Navy Hospital tomorrow, or as soon as you can manage the flight."

"Okay then, let's cut through the fucking bullshit from here on, Doc. Where is Komodo?"

Fox drilled his gaze on me a full minute as he responded in a short, cryptic tone of voice.

"When we got back to the main road, I took the woman in question into the bush, and I fired three rounds from my .45. The marine driver will verify that, and you can check the magazine for that matter. The weapon is now in your tent, on your rack, by the way."

I couldn't really move much, but I rolled my eyes at his pitifully lame answer—as if I were in any shape to jump up from the hospital bed right now and double time over to my tent. Then I'd count out the bullets in the magazine, and that would prove what to me?

"Oh come on, Chaplain or Doc, you are about being a life-saver either way you look at it. You are not a life-taker because that cuts across your grain; it always has been, and I'm sure it will always be. You let Komodo go, didn't you, Doc? You know I have to make a report of this, so don't keep blowing smoke up my ass. You just tell me what took place out there without all the happy tap-dancing. If we continue to get reports of the Komodo killing captured marines, that fucking blood will stain your hands for the rest of your life. I assume you are willing to live with that?" I was pretty groggy, but I was still pissed.

John stood up quickly from the chair and walked over toward the window, looking out at nothing in particular. He kept his back toward me as he spoke again. This time I could see the stress in his stance as he attempted to keep his composure.

"Ya know something, Gunny? Sometimes you are just too cynical for your own damn good. I just told you that I fired three rounds from my .45, and the woman that was our POW does not exist anymore. What more do you want from me?" He turned toward me, pointing his finger at me as he said, "You have *no* confirmation or knowledge that she was in fact the Komodo Dragon, and I have it on good authority that Komodo is much younger than the woman that we captured."

Now I was getting really pissed, and I tried to sit up. Between the meds and the pain, I decided that wasn't going to work very well. I was still out of it, but I needed some factual answers from him.

"You're full of shit, Doc, because you have no idea of what her age is. All information regarding Komodo is classified, and you don't have the goddamn need to know that. Stop blowing smoke at me! Damn it all to hell, Doc, we have been close, and we each owe our lives to the other person, but this just slams shut the door for us.

"My entire career as a marine is at stake here, and all because of this one mission. Now I could very well get a court martial because of what went down out there. I have compromised a top-secret mission and disobeyed a direct order; you do grasp that, don't you?

"I don't know if the mission was successful or not, and I can't even truthfully report that Komodo or some other mysterious and mythical sniper is dead. I just know that we had her once, and now we don't."

As John started to speak, I interrupted, "I'm sorry, Chaplain, but you and I as friends have reached the last page of the book. Go on and tend to your gullible flock, because you and I are finished, right here and right now! We were brothers out there and then you come back and fuck me over—for what? It's my ass that is hanging out, and you refuse the information that could cut me a huss.

"Fuck it, John, Doc, or Chaplain … *Ra kho cuoc song cua toi va o ngoai!*"[128]

---

[128] "Get out of my life and stay out from now on!"

Chapter 21

John was waving his hands around in obvious despair as he moved toward the door to leave the hospital room. He hesitated for a moment, and then he turned back around, pointing and shaking his finger at me again.

"Gunny Mac, you are forgetting one very important thing—in spite of everything that you just said, you full well know that I have to make a full mission report about this incident also. We were able to pull off a fast one on your commanding officer, and all for a good cause, I might add. The fact is that I went with you on this mission, and I took an active role by doing so. You want to make this sound as if this was your very own personal mission of do or die. Well, it wasn't your personal mission, because I was there and I had as much of a role in this mission as you did. You need to accept my role and that means my part was everything that yours was.

"I might also suggest that you make your report extremely accurate, Perry, because mine will articulate all of the events, and they'll be concise. Now that you have shot your mouth off, you can go on and ask the intel people if you can read my report and my version of the events that took place out there. You know what, Gunny? You never have asked me about anything; you just made your own weak-ass assumptions. You then have the audacity to berate me for not being a cold-blooded killer like you are. This is a war where it is our job—our duty—to kill other human beings, but there is also a sick pleasure that is derived from fulfilling your own personal vendettas. You have either forgotten, or you never did give a damn about another human being except for yourself.

"Good luck in the future, Gunnery Sergeant McMullin, and try thanking God for our lives, because we didn't do any of this completely on our own." He then made a perfect military about-face and walked briskly out of the door. I sorta expected John to look back and wave good-bye or something, but he just picked up his pace and walked straight ahead, slamming the outside door behind him.

Of course, I had knowingly spared John the second and most critical part of the mission; he had no idea that I was ordered to eliminate any possibility of that aviator falling into the hands of the North Vietnamese Army. In all probability, once in Hanoi, that officer would have been interrogated by the KGB or taken directly to the USSR. John didn't know that, because I didn't or couldn't tell him, and I don't think he would have been a part of the mission had he have known. I didn't have that choice, or I think that I would have passed too. It just was out of line for me to have to assassinate an American pilot because he got shot down and survived—but orders are, in fact, orders.

It still pissed me off to no end that Doc would not tell me the truth about the woman sniper, though. Of course she was somewhat older than the intelligence information had indicated about Komodo. But then again, intel is always screwing up something that is approximate and not always completely accurate.

It sucked that we had to part company on such a sour note, but this was all Doc's doing and not mine. So it is, and so it shall be!

No matter what, the ages of the women were close enough for military specs, and this one was really as good a shot as Komodo was reported to be. Besides, in spite of my having spoken to her in Vietnamese, she only glared back at me with utter contempt and hatred. She never spoke a single word to me, and that alone had to be some sort of a confession as to who she really was.

War very seldom makes for lifelong friends, and this was a classic disagreement between warriors regarding the direction things should go. The problems of where the ax would fall and whose head would roll in the end still remained. I didn't intend to piss away my career and life ambition as a sacrificial lamb for anyone.

In spite of what John said, it was, in fact, my mission from the very get go and while he played an active role; it was my report that counted the most. I was the trigger, and he was the spotter, so the bottom line was that I killed two of the enemy while he captured one and then apparently let her go. *O ngo ai lam tinh Hai quan dung con trai!*[129]

The following morning, I was loaded onto an Air Force medical evacuation aircraft to begin the long trip back to the States for corrective surgery to my shoulder. The bullet had tumbled as it entered my shoulder and therefore had screwed up considerable tissue and circulation from my shoulder to my arm. The doctor said that, if the damage wasn't repaired soon, my left arm could be jeopardized, and that, in time it would possibly have to be amputated.

Of course, that would also end my career in the marines, so away I went to Balboa Naval Hospital in San Diego, California.

I wasn't sure how I was going to get the word of my wound and my current location to my loving wife, Sarah. I had a phone number for Master Sergeant Adams someplace in my tent, but, unfortunately, my tent was still in Vietnam, and I wasn't. In a few days, I'll have someone start making some phone calls to the MPs in Saigon. Ken would be able to go to her house for me and bring her

---

[129] Outstanding there, navy boy!

up to date. Now I would have to coordinate all of my efforts from San Diego to try and get her back stateside. Damn it! I get married to the love of my life and I get shot a few days later. My thoughts of Sarah occupied my mind throughout most of the flight, but I was worried about how I could arrange for her to come to the United States now. This was all a strange feeling for me, because I never had to worry about a woman before. Now a woman was my wife, whom I loved with a burning passion that I never even knew existed within me. She was Vietnamese, and she was still in Saigon Vietnam, while I was almost an ocean away and on my way to another hospital in another country. I tried to recall what she said to me before the operation—she said something about a family. Was it about her family? We have no family together; it is just the two of us.

Before I left country, I was not advised if the mission had gone off as planned, or of what ultimately transpired after I was hit. Secrets and security are all so necessary to the well-being of our country, but I really felt that I was entitled to some closure on this particular mission. I sure as hell wasn't going to be contacting any Soviet agent and spilling my guts from a US Naval hospital bed.

If it did finish as planned, I'd be a hero of sorts, and if it didn't, I'd be the scapegoat and possibly be court-marshaled. Someone usually had to be found at fault when things turned bad, and you can bet your ass it wouldn't be one of those high-ranking brass assholes that came up with the impossible mission in the first place.

Wars are started by politicians and then planned by generals, but eventually they will be fought by kids who are young, dumb, and full of cum. They have to be young, because the older a person gets, the less they are willing to die without question. We are all supporting the politicians who think they need to back their stupid political party rather than think and vote for themselves. I love my country enough to give my life for her, but I detested the political involvement in the Vietnam War.

Split-second decisions that must be made out in the field are then second-guessed over a period of months by some REMF. They would then analyze the facts to see if we chose and did what was correct during that fraction of a second; it was almost always that fraction of a second that stood between your own life and someone else's death.

Second-guess my career and my life after the fact, you civilian, rear-echelon mother*fuckers*! Cut cho nhu ng nao con nguoi.[130] Civilians running a war is sorta like a flea having sex with a damn elephant!

It was a long flight back to the real world, but at least this time I had a bed to lie in and some excellent chow provided by the air force. The nursing care on the ride back was even better than it was back in the base hospital because it was impossible for the doctors and nurses to leave us. If they wanted to go someplace, it wasn't very far away, and someone was always there, attending to the needs of the wounded.

Can anyone ever applaud the beauty and compassion of a military doctor, nurse, or corpsman enough to truly say thank you for my life and limbs?

The airplane landed at Travis Air Force Base with all of the army and air force wounded being taken off of the aircraft first. There were also twelve caskets that had been loaded on board for the long ride home and then to their ultimate destination. I watched closely as the silver boxes with American flags covering them were silently offloaded by an honor guard.

I began thinking of all the men I had served with and known, many of whom returned home dead, crippled, or deformed. I think that was the first time I cried openly as an adult, and it wasn't just a few tears trickling down my face; it was sobbing that I couldn't control. They had each done a thankless job for a thankless nation—a

---

130 Shit for brains people.

price that was paid in full with each man giving all they had to give. Young lives were cut short by the sheer stupidity of this war.

From Travis Air Force Base, I was put on board a navy C-130 that would then be flown south to Naval Air Station North Island, which is basically in San Diego harbor.

My one surgery eventually turned into five, but I was finally reassembled and released back to limited duty. After four months of rehab and physical therapy, I was almost as good as when I was first issued to my corps of marines.

During my time at Balboa Hospital, I was able to get hold of Ken, and he, in turn, conveyed to Sarah what had happened. He called me back to tell me that she had been given the news, and that she would write to me as soon as possible. All of that sounded great to me, and I was overjoyed, knowing that Sarah was now in the loop.

"Here, Perry, hang on for a second, because I have an important news flash for you."

There was a brief silence before I heard the soft, sweet, sexy voice of my darling wife. "Hello, my husband, how are you? Kenny told me that it was okay for me to come to his office any time I wanted to speak with you on his telephone."

There were absolutely no medications that could have done for me what the sound of Sarah's voice did at that moment.

"He is also going to send you my letters through your mail system, so you will get them sooner. I sent you the photographs that we took when we were together, and I miss you so much, my blue-eyed marine."

I could hear Ken in the background whispering to her, "Tell him! Tell him, Sarah."

"*Chung ta se co mot em be chong bien cua toi,*"[131] Sarah said. "I

---

131 "We are going to have a baby, my Marine husband."

just found out the other day, and I had a dream where I saw you and I talked to you in this dream, my love. God was going to take you away from me, but I held on tightly to you so he couldn't have you at that time, my marine."

"A baby!" I shouted. "Sarah, you're pregnant?" My mind was reeling, because I might have imagined myself as married at some point and time, but … a baby? I just hoped it was a girl that looked like her mother. I was going to be a father with the most beautiful wife a man could have! This was a whole new side of me that I guess I had never imagined fitting into. I know that Sarah would be a wonderful mother, but there were so many questions without answers to still be answered regarding me. I wanted to be a father, and the to be best that I could possibly be.

After that day, we were able to speak to each other two or three times a week, and I got several letters keeping me abreast of her condition. Sarah said that she'd had a dream that the baby was a girl and that she had blue eyes like mine. I'd never seen a Vietnamese with blue eyes before, but Sarah was convinced that her dream was real. I had Ken get me the necessary documentation of Sarah's pregnancy, so hopefully this would expedite the paperwork to get her here.

Chapter 22

Limited duty, for me, was as an instructor back at Marine Corps Base, Camp Pendleton. This is the home of the First Marine Division Sniper School, where I had started out somewhere that seemed like it was about one hundred years ago.

When I arrived and checked into headquarters, Headquarters Battalion, I was summoned to make the morning formation the following day to be awarded the Silver Star and another Purple Heart.

Apparently, the word had finally filtered down that the SEALs and Force Recon guys were able to make a clean sweep of the POW camp. That was after the two sentries in the tower had been neutralized by the unbeatable team of the Cross and Sword, that is.

All three of the Americans were recovered, as were an additional six valuable NVA POWs. I was also told that the three pilots were supposed to have been moved toward Hanoi later that very same day, so our timing was, in fact, extremely crucial.

I'd already been told about being awarded the Silver Star while at the hospital, but apparently it had gone to Marine Corps Base Pendleton and seemed to be lost in the paperwork shuffle someplace. I figured it was no big deal, and that we'd meet up at some point.

There is no doubt that a Silver Star is a very prestigious decoration and not to be scoffed at, so I knew that we would be united.

Lieutenant Junior grade John Henry Fox, Chaplain, United States Navy was also presented a Silver Star and a promotion from ensign to lieutenant junior grade on December 21, for heroism against the enemy on a classified combat mission.

He was off the hook too, because the mission sorta went as planned. It isn't very often you'll see a chaplain wearing a medal for courage and valor, but, in this case, it was perhaps way past due. He should have received at least a Bronze Star and the Navy Commendation; both with *V*s from his first tour of duty.

The Navy Commendation Medal for saving men's lives is pretty damn lame, if you asked me—but then no one ever did, and I'm sure no one ever will either.

In the classified report, which I was never privileged to see, Fox stated that, after I was flown out, he talked to the female sniper, and that she spoke to him using near-perfect English with a slight French accent. She stated that her name was Hung, but she was code-named *Ho phu nu*, or Tiger Woman, a sniper for the Viet Minh, Viet Cong, and the Army of North Vietnam for the past twelve years.

She could speak, read, and write French, Cambodian, English, Chinese, and Vietnamese fluently, and often interpreted for captives and official government functions. She was adamant when she stated that she was never involved in the torture of Americans like the Komodo Dragon.

Tiger Woman said that she had actually met the Komodo Dragon twice before, and she had given John intelligence to pass along to our people. This invaluable information would provide the only real insight to what and to who she really was.

Komodo was a captain in the NVA and was apparently feared by everyone, regardless of their rank or standing, even within her own army. That is how she earned the name *Nhung phu nu ma tra tan va nhung su giet voi long khao khat.*

Any male found deserting from the Viet Cong or North Vietnam Army would also be subjected to the same treatment she gave our marines, except their death was much quicker. Her final comment was that Komodo would never be taken captive, because she continued to be surrounded by hundreds of soldiers at any given time.

Ho Phu Nu said that she would contact Fox at a later date and provide him with photographs and additional information on this cold-blooded killer.

Of course, Hung owed her life to Chaplain Fox, but she also hated the Komodo Dragon for her ongoing acts of inhumanity to any American males that she encountered.

Classified information can only be disseminated on a need-to-know, or eyes-only basis, and I was no longer in the loop to know what he had been told or done. Of course, I was unaware of that, and so I then too became a casualty of the unknown.

After Doc wrote his statement regarding the events of November 21, he was visited by Colonel Pensoneau, the commanding officer involving all Special Operations in I Corps, RVN.

Along with the colonel was Major Russ Mathews, United States Army Intelligence, from MACV/CICV/CDEC/CMEC in Saigon. This guy took the war very personally, and he was asking Bob leading questions about Tiger Woman and Komodo. He thought that Hung had duped both of us that day and that they really were, in fact, one and the same person.

His point and opinion were based on intel information, or the lack of it, regarding Tiger Woman. He said there was no record of her with the Viet Cong or the Army of North Vietnam. If there was another English-speaking female sharpshooter, his people would have found out about her a long time ago, so Komodo and Tiger

Woman absolutely had to be one and the same person, just as I thought they were.

Major Mathews also wanted to make an issue of a navy chaplain going along on the combat mission, but the colonel soon put a halt to the open-ended and accusatory questions that were being tossed about.

"Major Mathews, I know you have a job to do, and the intelligence that you so vigorously gather may or may not be of any real use to my marines out in the field, but let me establish this for you, Major. You will not come up here from Saigon like some grandiose wizard of knowledge and try to badger one of my marines. We are not intimidated by spooks!

"You have a copy of both reports that are now complete with factual and truthful statements and details. So now, Major, you are dismissed."

"But, Colonel I need to …"

"Major Mathews, you are now dismissed! Go and catch your airplane back to the Emerald City at Oz where your smoke and mirrors make your day, while good marines are dying for their country."

When the major had departed, the colonel turned to John and said, "Chaplain, you are quite aware that you stuck your neck out more than a mile on this one. I know your intentions were pure and that you wanted to take Gunny McMullin's six once again. It's hard to break a bond between two warriors, but please, don't ever make me cover your butt like this again.

"You richly deserve that Silver Star, Chaplain, because both of you did your duty and exceeded all that was ever expected of you—one more time."

Colonel Pensoneau then asked John, "I wonder, do you speak Latin, Chaplain?"

Fox smiled and said that he was a Baptist Minister, so he was able to skip that class.

"I expect you did," the colonel smiled back.

"Chaplain, I am a studier of the Roman Empire, and, in particular, their army. They didn't give medals to their soldiers, but the commanders did recognize the men who were found to be far and above the rest of the soldiers, or for those who showed bravery in battle. In some cases, they were promoted to an *aquilifier*, *optio*, or a *duplicarius*. In English, that would be the Legion standard- or eagle-bearer, the second noncommissioned officer in charge, or a soldier that received twice the pay of other soldiers. No matter which of those things came to fruition, the *legatus legionis*, *tribunus laciclavius*, or the *praefectus* would go through the camp, seeking out each soldier to be recognized. In the presence of his peers that were gathered about, he would honor that man by placing his hand on the left shoulder, close to the soldier's heart.

"Fortes fortuna adiuvat," he would proclaim, thus giving that soldier the honor and the respect of all that was Rome. That Latin phrase means 'Fortune favors the brave,' chaplain, and it certainly did just that for the two of you.

"However, I expect that, with McMullin gone, your days of going along on classified missions are over, and, the next time I hear anything more coming from you, it will be during Sunday services. I sincerely hope that I am correct on that, chaplain."

"Excuse me another moment, Colonel. As long as my neck is stretched way out there, may I ask a favor of you?"

"What is on your mind, Chaplain?" Colonel Pensoneau seemed anxious to end his conversation and get on with his schedule.

"Sir, as you're aware, neither of us would have come back alive from the mission without that misguided PFC showing up in that radio jeep. I was wondering if I could have the pleasure of rewarding him with a meritorious promotion to a lance corporal. I'm not sure if that would be the same as the *aquilifier*, *optio*, or *duplicarius*, but it would be something for him. There was no medal in it for him and no reward, except the threat of being disemboweled should he ever speak of the events that took place on that day."

Without hesitation, Colonel Pensoneau laughingly said, "I agree, and I'll make the necessary arrangements later on, Chaplain. Go to our admin office tomorrow and see the first sergeant: he will arrange to have that PFC promoted. One last thing, Chaplain, a lance corporal is nothing like those three names you just butchered the Latin names of."

"Well, Colonel, I was hoping that I might actually be able to do the promotion myself. You understand, of course, sir, just so that I may reinforce the code of silence to him personally."

"That's actually some pretty shameful bullshit coming from you, Chaplain, but of course you can promote him because you are an officer."

Later the next morning, John went directly to the admin office to see the first sergeant and explain the situation to him.

"It's okay, Padre. The colonel has already signed the promotion warrant, so all I need is the marine's full name and service number."

John waited for the warrant to finish being typed, and then he had a jeep and driver dispatched to get him. First Sergeant Effinger said, "Here ya go, sir; you're good to go. Are you going to wait for a formation to present it?"

That wasn't possible under the circumstances, but I could not explain that to him either.

"No can do, First Sergeant Effinger. The nature of this promotion is classified, so there won't be any formation at all, but thanks for your help." As he waited for the driver and jeep, he took out the paper from the envelope and read it.

To all who shall see these present, greetings. Know Ye that reposing special trust and confidence in the fidelity and abilities of Private First Class William Coker, I do hereby promote him to Lance Corporal ...

And it went on.

"It will come as a complete surprise for him to see me again, this time as a navy officer, and as a Chaplain to boot. I felt this was at least one tiny and positive moment in the war where something good could be returned in kind."

The jeep arrived at the admin office of H&S Company, First FSR, just a short drive later.

"I'd be looking for PFC Ronald L. Coker,"[3] John said.

"He is probably at chow, sir. I can have the runner go over to the chow hall and fetch him here for you if you'd like. Is everything okay with him, sir? I mean is everything okay stateside for him?"

"Oh, sure. I know this must look pretty solemn, with a chaplain coming here and looking for him, but I'm actually wanting to speak with him regarding another matter."

"Well, sir, I can have the runner take you over to the chow hall if you'd like."

John didn't want to make a big scene out of this, so he opted to walk over to the mess tent on his own.

PFC Coker was sitting with two other marines at a small table. "Good morning, marines. May I have you step outside with me for a moment, PFC Coker?"

John later said that he didn't think that he had seen a look of fear on a person's face like Coker had at that moment. He just sat there, staring at him with his mouth wide open.

"Sir, *honest*, I didn't say anything to anyone because if I'm in trouble ..."

"You're not in trouble, Coker, and I'm quite sure you have maintained the required level of confidentiality. Outside for a moment, please?"

When they walked away from the mess tent, Coker said, "You really are a sir, but you are in the navy, and you are a chaplain. Is that for real, or is that like some secret or undercover thing you guys do, sir?"

John tried to suppress his smile as he continued, "I told you that this entire matter or even a minute part of it may never be discussed, right?"

"Yes, sir, you sure did, and honest, sir, I never said anything to anyone, so help me, sir."

They stopped in the shade of a tent as John turned toward this very nervous marine. "PFC Coker, by your showing up that day, you saved the lives of three people. Why in heaven's name did you turn off of the main road and come all of the way up to where we met?"

Coker said, "I guess I don't know the answer to that, sir. I didn't think about it really. It was almost like someone turned the steering wheel for me. It's strange, sir, because that was something I would have never have done then, and I would never do now. Is that what I'm in trouble for?"

"You are not in any trouble, at least not as of yet. I was going to ask for you to be presented with a commendation medal for your actions that day, but medals have to say why they were given to someone. We couldn't very well put 'classified' on yours, now could we?"

As PFC Coker was shaking his head no, John handed him two lance-corporal rank devices for the collar of his uniform. Coker looked at them for several seconds, not understanding exactly what was taking place.

John smiled as he said, "I would pin these on for you, Lance Corporal, but I don't want people seeing that and then asking you a bunch of questions. In this envelope is your promotion warrant, which makes all of this official. I'm sure you will be asked by many people about your sudden and secret promotion, so there is a letter in here for your commanding officer, and that will explain all of the things he is required to know.

"This entire matter is still top secret and will remain so for about a hundred years or something close to that. When you are asked questions by your fellow marines, just tell them it is classified information, and you will not discuss it with them.

"But should they persist, you can tell them that they can go and ask your commanding officer for the details if they feel the need to know more about it. Once again, Lance Corporal Coker, those stripes can go away, so remember, 'Loose lips sink ships.'"

"Aye, sir. So, I'm confused. Did I actually see and talk with you here today?"

"The only person you saw today was an undercover intelligence person or something like that, and that's the end of that conversation. It remains a top-secret thing and, once again, thanks again for the ride home that day." John shook his hand and turned away to walk back to the admin office. After a few steps, he turned back to speak to a still-confused marine who was still looking at the chevrons in his hand. "*Fortes fortuna adiuvat*, and congratulations once again on your promotion." Fox then walked back to the company office with a huge smile on his face.

Chapter 23

John was sitting in the tiny office of the chapel, still in deep thought about his Sunday sermon, when a female voice came from behind him, breaking his concentration.

"'Scuse me, mister sir, you please be the Chaplain Fox John?" Mama San asked. The woman was very small and withered, but wearing the oversized black pajamas favored by the poor and working class of Vietnam. As she spoke, she slid her straw, cone-shaped hat off of her head, exposing a deep, six-inch scar above her ear. John silently wondered which side she was fighting for when she obtained that zipper.[132]

"Yes, I am. How may I help you?" he replied.

"My name Ong. I come speak here for Hung. You know her name become Tiger Woman," she whispered.

"Yes, *yes*, of course I do, I know her. Where is she? Can I see or talk to her?" John was looking past her, hoping that Tiger Woman would come walking down the aisle of the makeshift church. That was when he noticed the woman speaking to him was not wearing the required security pass for a worker or visitor. Apparently, she

---

132 Visible wound

knew where we had a hole in our parameter and she had managed to scamper through it. She had likely done this before, and she could probably do it anytime she wanted to.

Ong said that Hung was close by, but she was hiding from her many enemies.

"Now, so many people want to be seeing Hung be died. You army, she army, everybody in army look for her now making wish dead on her. Very bad, you see, sir. *Ho deu muon cat co hong cua minh de khong bao gio noi chuyen mot lan nua.*"[133]

John wondered, why the NVA would be looking for her, and he got the point. "Ong when and where can I talk with Hung?"

Ong handed him a piece of paper with just the words "Lucky Bar" written on it.

"Hung be at Lucky Bar tomorrow at ten o'clock morning time. You go first, then she come see you after she see you, not followed. You no stay then at Lucky Bar, cause you need go more secret place for talk. You *hieu*,[134] Chaplain?"

"Yes, I understand, I *hieu* what you say, Ong. I will be at the Lucky Bar tomorrow at ten a.m. *Cam on ban, Ong.*"[135]

*   *   *

John walked into the Lucky Bar just before ten and was immediately ushered into a back room, where they were cooking something that smelled like rubber burning.

He sat down, and, after a few minutes, a girl about eleven or twelve years old arrived and took him by the hand, pulling John up and onto his feet. Obviously, she was not full-blooded Vietnamese,

---

133 "They all want to cut her throat so she can never speak again."
134 "Understand"
135 "Thank you, Ong."

because she appeared to be partly Caucasian and had light-blue eyes.

"Please come with me, Reverend. I will guide you to someplace near here."

They went out the back door and down a small alley to another door that led into another bar. This one was enclosed with a grenade fence that was securely locked.

After considerable chattering, everyone quickly dissipated as Hung appeared from within a shadow. The young girl remained as they sat down in a hidden booth.

Without speaking, Hung handed John a sealed packet and motioned for him to open it. There were three eight-by-ten, black-and-white photographs within. The first photo one was that of a woman who was obviously dead. Her head was swollen and distorted, with a small black hole in her forehead. It was obviously an entry wound from a gunshot.

The next picture was of the same woman when she was younger and dressed in a black *ao dai.*

There was a third photograph of her wearing the officer's uniform of the North Vietnamese Army.

John looked questioningly at Hung while he was holding the pictures toward her.

With no visible emotion, she pointed to the first picture and said, "This is *Nhung phu nu ma tra tan va nhung su giet voi long khao khat.* She is now the Komodo Dragon woman that I have killed. Although she was much hated and feared, I am hunted because of her now too.

"This is my daughter Phuong, Chaplain Fox. Please sit with her for a few moments, and I will return back here soon. There is someplace I must quickly go."

Hung stood up, still holding John's hand. Tears were welling up in her eyes, and they began streaming down her cheeks. She started to speak to him a couple of different times, but, as she tried to say something, she would begin to sob. A moment later, she turned and literally ran out the back door.

Phuong and John sat nervously without speaking for a couple of minutes. "How long will your mother be gone, Phuong?" John finally stammered.

"My mother cannot return ever in this time for me, Chaplain Fox. She say for me to stay with you, and maybe I can go to America with you as my father. My Vietnam name is Phuong, but please, you will call me by Fawn if I am ever to remain with you, Mr. Fox."

"Come on, Phuong, let's go and look for your mother. She can't have gone very far away this quickly." John stood, looking toward the door Hung had disappeared through.

Phuong took both of John's hands while pulling him back toward her. She looked absolutely terrified of what they would meet up with if they were to leave.

"We cannot go from here for now, my reverend. My mother is hunted by many, many bad people that will kill her, and if we are there with her, they will most gladly kill us also. My mother say for us to stay one hour here before we leave from this place; please sir. *Xin!*"[136]

They were brought some hot tea that tasted like soapy water and sticky rice balls, complete with weevils that were wrapped in banana leaves. John said he was thinking that right now a shot of Jack Daniels would serve him a lot better than lousy tea and bug-infested rice.

"Phong, why did your mother kill Komodo if she knew what was going to happen to her afterward? She had to know that the result for killing her would mean that she'd also be hunted down and killed."

---

136 *"Please!"*

"Yes, of course she knew. The Komodo Dragon was evil to all men alike, but Americans she hates most than even the French soldiers.

"My mother believes in God, Chaplain, because we are Catholic. My mother saw Komodo as very evil, and she saw even more because of your kindness for her. Because she believed that God sent you to her, she struck the Komodo woman down so no other man would ever suffer from her again. It was your kindness that changed my mother from killing more men in your army of marines and then to kill the one person that was very, very evil.

"My mother was once married to a French major. He was an advisor to our country, but in his military. He often would beat my mother, so she was bruised from him. One night when he was very drunk and with two of his friends, they each took turns using my mother, and then they laughed at her pain. From the night of those three men with her, I became born to my mother. Those men were very evil also, but our police would do nothing to them, because they were French officers.

"My mother is a kind heart, chaplain, but they had done great harm to her. One night soon after that, they went to a drinking party on a boat at the harbor. They were never seen again coming from there. And then my mother was hunted by our own police for their sad accident. She took me to a safe village to be raised by *cua nu tu,*[137] and they educated me well, but I seldom get to see my mother that I love.

"From that time after, she became a Viet Minh to be safe away from our police. My mother said now came her time to pay back to God for her sins also, but she should have to have killed the Komodo Dragon woman first.

"I understand that you cannot take me to America along with

---

137 "Nuns"

you, Mr. Fox, and the nuns expect me to return back with them tonight. Now, it is safe for us to leave here, but first I think you need to burn the pictures that my mother gave to you, because it would be very bad if you were seen with them.

"Now, I go back to my village, the nuns, and my school. Good-bye, and thank you for believing in and trusting my mother. Please pray for us, please, Reverend Fox."

PART TWO: PHAN HAI

Chapter 24

"Sergeant Major McMullin, *hoac toi se goi cho ban*[138] Zapper? Perhaps Ghost Rider is more fitting—or shall it be just Chime Whiskey? They each still fit you after these many years don't they, *nuuoi ban cu cua toi ban tia?*"[139]

I was stunned to hear those old war tags, but even more so the voice from my past. I knew immediately that it was Chaplain John Henry Fox.

"Well, look at you, Chaplain. A navy three-stripe lieutenant commander now? That Silver Star must have pushed you right up the ladder during these past few years?"

John smiled as he shook my hand. "You have done well yourself—sergeant major of the Fifth Marine Regiment. Can I talk you into having some warm tiger piss with me? And this time, I'll be the one buying."

Today was supposed to be an uneventful run to the PX for me, and I had business up the yin yang that I had to attend to immediately after lunch. "Let me make a call to my boss, Lieutenant

---

138 "Or shall I call you Zapper?"
139 "My old sniper friend?"

195

Commander, and you're on—but remember, it's your tab, and that goes for the chow later on too."

It had now been several years from the time I was medevaced from Da Nang, and Doc or Chaplain or whoever the hell he was and I parted company under some very strained circumstances. He had called and sent a few letters, but I just felt that was all behind me … us … so I never got back to him. Perhaps it is something in my hardheaded and stubborn Scottish blood.

We settled for a nice, quiet restaurant in Oceanside, located at the end of the pier. We stayed and talked, unaware of the time, until they kicked us out at 2200 hours.

"I have kept abreast of your career from gunny to sergeant major, Perry. You did two more tours in Vietnam with your receiving another Silver Star, which I understand should have actually been the Navy Cross. And then a Bronze Star, another Purple Heart, and many, many more ribbons and medals. I'd say you did quite well as far medals go, but what about the price that you have personally paid?

"I'm guessing that you're not so different from the many other people that returned home from Vietnam to find that the war wasn't stuffed away quite as neat and as tidy as you thought it was. Aside from that excess baggage, so many are suffering from the effects of PTSD, dioxin, carcinogens, and Lord knows what else. There are no medals given out for those injuries.

"And your shoulder—how is the shoulder wound holding up these days?"

I wanted to address the unfinished business that was left over from a time that was behind us. I said, "I sort of got the story about what actually went down after I was taken away by dust off that day, John. I was completely out of line by saying what I did to you back then, but how was I to know that you had obtained further information that was classified even to me?

"But one thing I do know, Commander Fox—Komodo just

completely disappeared from the face of the earth after that day, so I still wonder, was she or wasn't she that woman we captured?"

"Well, Sergeant Major, I may have some insight to that question for you. The problem is, that if I tell you, I may have to kill you!" It was such a lame joke, but it still had merit within the right circles. It actually spoke volumes about what had been or would be said.

We sat and talked like we had done before—as friends should do. John told me that he had been married once, but then they divorced after four years and another tour in Vietnam. A year away in a combat zone was always rough on a woman, a marriage, and the family.

My voice began to tremble as I spoke, "Yeah, I was married once too, John. She was the most gorgeous woman in all of Vietnam, and I loved her so very, very much." I told him the story of how we had met and our short, but sweet, wedding. When he asked me why I hadn't told him anything of Sarah before the mission, I said that all we had time for back then was the critical assignment at hand. Besides, I wanted to show him the photographs of Sarah while I was telling him the story.

"So what became of Sarah and your daughter?" John hesitantly asked.

I took another deep breath and tried to speak, but my voice began trembling again, and tears began welling up in my eyes. When I was finally able to talk, I looked away from him. "Both Sarah and our baby daughter were killed by a rocket that was indiscriminately fired into Saigon. The immigration papers that we had been waiting for—the ones that would have brought both Sarah and our baby home to the United States—had finally just been approved. They were on their way to go shopping for their trip back to the States when the rocket took both of them, her parents, and her sister out. They are now buried in the cemetery of the same Catholic church where we were married. They are still my wife and my daughter, you know, John. They are the only family I've ever wanted."

I told Fox that I'd received a letter from Sarah's brother, outlining the events as they took place that day. He'd asked if I could help him out with some money, because he needed to place a marker on their grave. Of course I gave him more money than was necessary for all of their expenses, and he sent me pictures once everything had been completed. Sarah and our daughter were buried in the same grave together, as a mother and her baby should be. Her brother had done very well for his and my beloved family.

"There is no fairness in any war, Chaplain, and I am well aware of that. Soldiers go into battle for various reasons, but my wife and my child were not soldiers and it wasn't even their war. What in the hell was the need of a rocket being fired into their part of her city?" As I spoke, tears welled up in my eyes again, and I just couldn't find the words that I needed to continue.

"There never was a reason for their death that I could manage to come up with. I had tried to reason out their deaths, but I never could, so eventually I successfully stuffed the pain and the memory away someplace. I thought they were buried and out of my memory so I could move on with my own life and duties.

"So, here I sit today with enough stripes on my arm to make a zebra envious, and I have hash marks all the way up to my frigg'n elbow. My house is still a lonely place, so I drink myself to sleep every night. Then I chase the booze with sleeping pills to keep the ugly dreams away. There are so many, many goddamn faces without names that I see in my dreams; they're driving me nuts. These people are fucking dead, so why do they keep haunting me?"

John knew that there was no answer to what I had just said. After pausing, he finally said, "Hey, Sergeant Major, I have something I'd like you to share with me this coming Friday—that is, providing you would care to come along with me for the entire evening. Well, in fact, I insist on it, and I'll pull rank if necessary to insure that you do come. I know the commanding general of the division by his first name, you know."

"Oh, give me a frigg'n break, Mr. High-and-Mighty Lieutenant Commander. I know his first and his *middle* name, you asshole. So what's the event? Are you getting married again, and you want me to be your best man?"

"No, you original 1775 Tun Tavern veteran. I want to take you back to a time and a place when you were a gunnery sergeant, but you were still ... a world-class asshole.

"There will be no other clues available for you, so I'll pick you up at your house this Friday at 1700. Oh, and by the way, Sergeant Major of the Fifth Marines, please wear your dress blues, tennis shoes, and a light coat of oil, okay?"

"Cut me a huss, you salty old anchor-clanker; what's with the dress blues?"

"Because it is appropriate for the occasion, Sergeant Major, but only if you think you can manage to dress yourself, you crusty old barnacle."

I was wondering what the chaplain had up his three-striped sleeve for the rest of that day, and then Thursday, and then again on Friday. Whatever it was, he wasn't budging with any clues. It was great seeing him again, though—sort of like having been reunited with my brother, I suppose.

I left headquarters early to get home to shit, shower, and shave and then to put on my dress blues. No matter how many times I put that uniform on, I was always proud to look into the mirror and say that I was a marine that had served my country the best way I knew how. I didn't give a shit about the current or the past political picture. I went when and where my country asked me to go, and I always did the job I was trained to do. Sometimes my best may not have been good enough and sometimes doing my best meant that the enemy died while they were doing their best.

Semper Fi!

The chaplain showed up promptly at 1700. I asked him once

again what the drill[140] was for the dress blues because he was also decked out in his navy dress white uniform. The commander said this particular mission was considered confidential until after we had arrived at our destination.

"Then what is our destination?" I asked, still trying to break into a clue.

"Just wait a minute, and you'll see, for crying out loud! I swear, you are still like George Custer—you charge forward at full speed, and you'll face the consequences later. Just you hang on to your skivvies for a bit, okay ex-Gunny?"

I feared that he had set both of us up for some history speech or some kind of silliness that these college clowns wanted. "We don't have to stand up in front of a bunch of jerk-off civilian pukes and talk about a war that took place a long time ago, do we John? I only talk about the war if and when I am with other Vietnam veterans; not even with the marines that were never there. It's over, it's done, and I just don't like talking about it anymore, Commander."

"Hold on, Perry, don't get your feathers ruffled up just yet. I didn't set you up for anything like that—but first things first.

"I need to bring you up to date on something extremely important in fact it is crucial to set our record straight once and for all. By our record, I am talking about some bad karma that still exists between the two of us, and it has to be resolved before we can move on to something else here in just about forty-five minutes."

John had that look of determination on his face that was telling me our rift was going to be mended right here and right now.

As he was speaking to me, he pulled a worn envelope from under the sun visor. "Sergeant Major, this will take us back in time and hopefully resolve an issue regarding a woman that you believed to be the Komodo Dragon. Well, in fact, she was not Komodo, and I

---

[140] Reason

have known that since the day you were flown away by dust off so long ago. I think it is high time that I provide you with the proof you that you'll need to set this entire matter aside forever.

"Because of the entire NVA female-sniper thing, and specifically because of Komodo, this was classified as *bi mat dinh*,[141] so therefore I could never tell the truth; not even to you. I did not destroy these photographs after I was told to, and I recently received permission for them to be declassified. There are three eight-by-ten photographs in here that have been waiting to provide you with the answer you have been seeking for a long time."

I opened the envelope and removed three faded black-and-white photographs. The first was that of a woman wearing the traditional black pajamas of the Viet Cong. She was laid flat on her back with an entry wound from a bullet that was almost right smack dab between her running lights. From the distorted skull, I knew that she had been shot at close range with a high-powered rifle.

"These photographs are all of your real Komodo Dragon woman that a gunny by the name of McMullin vowed to kill at any cost. And, in many respects, you actually did kill her, because she was eventually taken out by that very same woman sniper that shot you. You were positive from the first moment that she was Komodo, and rightfully so, I guess. Even our own intel people did not know of the existence of the woman that we captured on that day.

"The woman that we captured that day was, in fact, code-named Tiger Woman or *Ho Phu Nu*, but her real name was Hung. The Komodo woman's real name never did come up, but *Nguoi ban cu cua toi ban tia* definitely died at the hands of Tiger Woman.

"Yes, indeed, Sergeant Major, I did in fact let her go free that day, because after you wanted so much to kill her, I saw her as another human being and not as my personal enemy. She would not speak

141 Top secret

to you that day because she knew that your mind was already made up, and that you would kill her anyway.

"At that time, she should have been my enemy also just for having shot you, but she was also a soldier like we were. So what if it had been you or I that was captured by them on that day? We didn't need to kill her just because they would have killed us if we had been captured by them.

"Because of that single act of kindness I showed, and by my letting her go free, she only ever fired one more shot in anger. That was to kill an evil woman known to you as the Komodo Dragon. The second photograph shows her in her officer's NVA uniform, and so I believe this is the proof you seek. Had you have killed Tiger Woman that day, how many more marines do you think would have died at the hands of that ruthless Vietnamese woman?"

My interest was now piqued, and I was beginning to actually feel sorry for Hung, who did for me what I vowed to do at any cost. "So, where is she? What happened to her for killing Komodo?" I asked John.

"About a week after you were sent back stateside, I met with and spoke to her. That is when she gave me these photographs. At that time, the entire Army of North Vietnam and the Viet Cong were hunting her. I never saw or spoke with her after that day, so I can only assume that she didn't live very long after she killed the woman that you hated so much."

"Thanks, Chaplain. I guess I have just learned a little something about compassion, hate, and forgiveness. I suppose too that I have carried this anger along with me for a long time, and that it has kicked my ass throughout my own attempts at love and relationships. I carried my anger for way too many years as I refused your phone calls and letters. I guess I can see now that was my loss."

John sat there a moment, reflecting on my words, before he spoke again. "Perry, it is never too late to say 'I'm sorry' to someone, and it is never a sign of weakness to seek comfort from another. You can also start to find your own level of comfort this Sunday, if you'd care to join me at church. I fear that my roof may cave in, but I'll chance that."

"John, I will start by saying I'm sorry to you for the anger I felt for way too many years now, and also to say thank you to you for being my friend. Before we go, I'd ask you to say a prayer for all of the men and women that served with us in Vietnam. Many of them were people we knew, and too many were people that we saw die or suffer from their wounds, suicides, and Agent Orange. Pray for them, Chaplain, because all of us are now part of a unique group of people that closed our club membership back in 1975."

I then added, "I'll ask one last favor of you, my friend. I guess I have been somewhat remiss about going to church. If I show up sometime, do you suppose you might dedicate a service in memory of my wife and daughter?"

John sat silently and shook his head up and down as he cried for the pain that he could feel coming deep with inside me.

Chapter 25

As we were walking from the car to the auditorium, the commander said, "Sergeant Major McMullin, if you'd please remain covered during the ceremony … you'll understand why in a little while now. Do you think you can follow my orders for just this one time, marine?"

"*Choi oi*, come on, Doc, I still outrank you because I'm a marine, and you are still just a chicken-shit swabbie, no matter how many stripes you have on your sleeve."

We both laughed, and I knew he would have been disappointed if I would have caved into him.

Several attempts to find out why we were at a college graduation went unanswered. The commencement began as soon as we sat down in our reserved seats.

"Perry, do you see that navy officer in her dress whites—the one getting ready to come up on the stage?"

"Sure I do; she sticks out like a sore thumb with all of those other college pukes in their black bathrobes. So what's your point?"

"Just shut up, listen, and watch then," John cryptically replied.

When it was the new ensign's time to go up and receive her diploma as a medical doctor in the United States Navy, they announced her name. It was Fawn Fox.

My head snapped to my right, and I looked at John, sitting there with a big grin on his face.

"What's going on here, Doc? And who is Fawn Fox? Is she related to you somehow?" I asked.

"Just pay attention, Perry, because she is actually related to both of us now," the commander sassed back at me.

As Ensign Fawn Fox received her diploma, she walked smartly to the end of the stage. Once there, she turned toward us and snapped a salute in our direction.

"She is not saluting me; she is saluting you, Sergeant Major, so please stand and return our daughter's salute."

I was in shock, but I managed to come to attention, and I returned the most important salute that has ever been rendered to me. She stood there, waiting for me, before she walked down the stairs and came toward us.

John said, "I don't share my daughter with you, Perry; she shares both of us. Hung, or Tiger Woman, was her mother."

"*Loi chao cuoi chin.*[142] When you were a marine gunnery sergeant in Vietnam, you could have killed my mother," Fawn said. "You didn't do that, and I am grateful to you now, Sergeant Major, because, while my mother was your hated enemy, you allowed her the final dignity that she alone chose.

"This man standing beside you is the only father I have ever known, and it is he that has given me my dignity and the pride to be who I am today. But you—you have also been in my heart and my thoughts for these many years, because you knew and believed in my mother also.

"Now I will call you *Cha Toi,*[143] if you will honor me so, Sergeant Major McMullin. After all, a young Vietnamese woman cannot

---

[142] "Hello at last."
[143] "My father."

possibly have too many good fathers—especially a father who has blue eyes the same as I do. Imagine that, Sergeant Major. Have you ever heard of a Vietnamese woman with blue eyes before?"

"Yes, indeed, Fawn. Actually I have known one other Vietnamese person that had blue eyes," I said softly.

What in the world had John told her? Had he taken my anger and replaced it with love for this innocent woman? Didn't he think that she needed to know the truth and the hate about the war that each one of us has shared? I glanced over at John with an obvious question on my face as tears began welling up in my eyes. Doc just nodded his head and smiled back at me knowingly—this being the man who had not harbored a grudge the way I had done for so many wasted years.

I hugged Fawn close to my chest and whispered into her ear, "*Toi se co vinh du duoc nguoi cha cua ban vang nhat, cam on ban nay. No co nghia la nhieu hon ban da ban gio co the trong tuong. Toi chng vinh du duoc yen em nhu toi en thuong con gai da duoc lay ta toi.*"[144]

With that said, the three of us joined arm in arm as we actually went skipping down the stairs and out of the auditorium. I'm sure this was very funny to the folks gathered there, because some were military, but even those who were not knew that military regulations did not include skipping. We must have appeared to be three crazy children from *The Wizard of Oz* who were rejoicing in newfound life and love. Indeed, we appeared very unmilitary, but then they couldn't exactly shave my head and send me to Vietnam for punishment now, could they?

The emotion, love, and pride were swelling and filling me just as the thoughts of my own child had become more and more persistent within my mind over these many years. It was never possible for me

---

144 "I will be honored to be your father, Fawn, and I thank you. It means more to me than you could ever imagine. I am honored to love you as I would have loved the daughter that was taken from me."

to get past my wife's and daughter's death, but now I know full well that they are just gone from this earth and not from within me. Someday, I would hope to join them—a family together at long last.

Moi nguoi trong chung ta da den vong day du thong qua ban be, ke thu cuoc song, cai chet, tinh yeu va noi buon.

Viet Nam la mot thoi gian va diem voi mot cuoc chien tranh trong thuc te no la mot cuoc chien tranh do la ngay hom qua mot lan nua![145]

Ket Thuc
The End

---

[145] Each one of us had come full circle through friends, enemies, lives, deaths, love, hate, and sorrow.
Vietnam was a time and a place with a war. In fact it was a war that was yesterday—once again today!

And then ...
The Final Chapter

Just eleven months after this joyous reunion, the sergeant major died from the cancerous effects of Agent Orange. He had hidden his disease from everyone except his closest friend, John Fox.

The Reverend John Fox was now the pastor at the Evangelista Pentecostal Church, where Perry had become a loyal parishioner, attending each and every Sunday with his daughter, Fawn.

Fawn and her marine husband had a baby boy one year later, whom she named Perry. Two years later, she would name her baby daughter Sarah.

John, Fawn, and her family eventually received permission to place Perry's ashes with his wife and daughter in Saigon, now Ho Chi Minh City, Vietnam. The three of them were finally together—a complete family at long last.

Fawn and John were unable to find any trace of Fawn's mother, Hung. They searched all known war records from both the North and South of Vietnam and even placed newspaper ads, hoping that someone who had known her would come forward. No one ever did.

Afterthoughts

P TSD: Sometimes there is no more room for us to stuff emotions and our feelings. Having a problem with any war is a natural thing for human beings. It's *not* having a problem with them that is not a human emotion. There is help available from the Veterans Administration, and you have nothing to lose.

Dioxin: It is the war that will not end for soldiers, sailors, marines, navy, and the coast guard that served in Korea and Vietnam. The people of Vietnam continue to have an extremely high rate of cancer and birth defects from the dioxins and carcinogens used by our government without regard to humanity. They continue to stalk and claim their victims decades after the last shots of the war were fired. There are tens of thousands of men, women, and children who have already died or will die from the effect from these so-called "safe" chemicals.

It is the continuing war of the rainbow of herbicide agents—orange, blue, green, and pink, white, and purple—the colorful rainbow of continuing death and suffering that was used in two different countries.

The Vietnam War: September 26, 1959, to April 30, 1975.

There were 58,267 Americans killed and 303,644 Americans

wounded. The number of Americans that served within the borders of South Vietnam from January 1, 1965, to March 28, 1973, was approximately 2,594,000. In the census of 2000, there were approximately 1,002,511 real Vietnam veterans. The number of Americans *claiming* to be Vietnam veterans was 13,853,027.

There will never be accurate numbers for how many Vietnamese died or were wounded. A guess would be around 2,270,000.

Authored by Staff Sergeant Perry V. McMullin, 1981844
United States Marine Corps December 1961 to December 1971